"The world is violent and mercurial—
it will have its way with you. . . .
We live in a perpetually burning building,
and what we must save from it,
all the time, is love."
—*Tennessee Williams*

"Love is a growing up."
—*James Baldwin*

The Ada Decades

PAULA MARTINAC

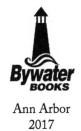

Bywater
BOOKS

Ann Arbor
2017

Introduction

This is a work of fiction, inspired in part by actual events, people, and places. Although Charlotte, North Carolina's public schools did experience racial strife in 1957 and 1970, Central Charlotte Junior High never existed; Mary Burney is not a historical figure, but an amalgam loosely based on the African-American students who integrated public schools in the South; and Robert Browne is a product of my imagination. I derived an understanding of events in Charlotte and places like Little Rock by reading the work of James Baldwin, Jim Grimsley, Thomas W. Hanchett, Davison M. Douglas, and David Margolick, and the coverage of school integration in the *Charlotte Observer*.

There was indeed a lynching of three African-American men in Salisbury, N.C., in 1906, and a postcard of the murdered men appears in the collection of WithoutSanctuary.org. But there are no shadowy children in the photo, and I changed the name of the photography studio on the back of the postcard. I owe my knowledge of this horrific event to the work of Susan B. Wells.

To my knowledge, there was no raid on a gay cruising area in Charlotte in April 1962; my chapter "The Plan" took its inspiration from many such incidents that occurred all over the United States in this time period. For my understanding of LBGT life in the South before Stonewall, I'm indebted to James T. Sears's oral histories. An exhibit at the Levine Museum of the New South in 2014"— "LGBTQ Perspectives on Equality"—helped inform my understanding of Charlotte's queer past.

Musical theater mavens, please forgive the small liberty I took with the date of *The Music Man*, which did not open on Broadway until December 1957— three months after Cam sang "Marian the Librarian" to Ada. The song was just too perfect to pass up.

Paula Martinac
Charlotte, NC

Private Things

1947

Ada's daddy kept a postcard of three dead colored men in his toolbox. He stashed it in the bottom well, under the removable tray, in a ratty, soiled envelope.

She had volunteered to fetch a wrench. At almost twelve, Ada took pride in knowing the difference between a wrench and pliers, because most girls her age didn't and her mother thought she shouldn't bother. "You won't need that when you're married," her mama, who wed at just seventeen, said. "That's what husbands are for."

If she hadn't decided to lift the tray, just for a peek, Ada wouldn't have noticed the envelope at all. It was wedged behind several boxes of nails, demanding investigation. It looked like half of North Carolina had handled it, so why shouldn't she? She tucked it into the inner pocket of her overalls, the one she had sewed in as a secret storage place, then delivered the wrench to her father.

"Good girl," her father said when she returned from the tool shed. He was on his back underneath the kitchen sink, attending to a leak that had been dripping for days. It used to be Clay Junior who assisted with these tasks, but Ada's older brother was too busy with basketball practice and other unspecified high school activities. Soon, her father would train Foster, the youngest, in the workings of the toolbox, but in the interim, Ada pitched in. She didn't mind—it was about the only time she spent with her father, who in his free time was less prone to talking than drinking, smoking on the porch and listening to shows like *Amos 'n' Andy*.

It occurred to her that if he put the wrench back himself, her daddy might miss the envelope and then he would whup her for sure. She figured she had no more than fifteen minutes in which to explore the contents of the envelope. She closed her bedroom door just partway so she could hear if he called to her again, and withdrew the ragged paper from her secret pocket.

The envelope held a strange assortment of items, including half a dozen dirty pictures of women, all with big bosoms exposed to the world and legs wide open. Their heads tilted in the same provocative way. One woman had no panties on and crossed her hands demurely over her privates.

The envelope also held a used bus ticket to Charlotte and two yellowed teeth. The ticket, she figured, might be the very one that brought her daddy to Charlotte in the '20s as a young man looking for work in the cotton mills. The teeth she let be, her curiosity not deep enough to prompt her to touch anyone else's teeth, even if, for some reason, they had once belonged to a member of her family.

And then, inside another thin, dirty sleeve was the postcard of the dead men.

At first, she wasn't sure what it depicted, but a closer look made her stomach pitch. One man was swinging from a tree by his neck and legs, almost like he was flying; his face seemed to be half gone. The bodies of the other two were slumped against the trunk. None of the men had shirts on, and their trousers were in tatters. To the right a white hand held up an unreadable sign, while a straw boater covered the owner's face. Almost out of frame were three small white blurry heads—children in motion. The postcard was stamped on the reverse, "From Carson's Studio, near Court House, Salisbury, N.C." Someone had scrawled an inscription, and the ink had faded to gray: *Remember this?*

Many of her extended family members, including her widowed grandmother, still lived in the farmlands just outside Salisbury. Her father had been the first Shook to leave, followed by his older brother a year later. He was just shy of twenty and had never been to a city. "He wanted a better life," her mama said.

2

"He didn't want to be scraping by like a field hand his whole life." At the Mercury Mill, he worked his way up to weave room overseer, which secured him a slightly larger house in the mill village and allowed Ada's mother to quit her job as a spinner at the same mill.

Ada heard her father stirring in the other room, sliding out from under the sink. "That 'bout does it, Janie!" he called out to Ada's mother. Ada stashed the postcard in her school bag and the dirty envelope back in her pocket. It was a risk to hold onto the card, but she would find some way to replace it before he missed it. She wondered how often he actually looked at the grisly thing, and if her mama knew about it.

"Let me put away that wrench for you, Daddy," Ada said, slipping it from his hand. "Why don't you sit down now, and I'll bring you a glass of cold tea?"

Clay Senior offered a rare smile. A hand went out to touch her hair, but it was slick with grease and he withdrew it before it made contact. "Well, aren't you the sweet one!" he said. "I knew there was a reason I call you Sugar."

In the tool shed, sweat broke out on Ada's upper lip when she couldn't remember whether the flap of the envelope had faced out, toward the boxes of nails, or in, toward the toolbox itself. She took a guess and then closed the top of the wretched thing with a thunk.

That night, she dreamed she was being chased by three brawny men, whose skin colors kept changing; she tried to scream, but nothing came out of her mouth. One man looked a little like her daddy, but then he didn't. She ran into a field where the bodies of white and colored children littered the landscape, and she woke up shrieking, her nightdress soaked in sweat.

Her mama hurried into Ada's room, still throwing on her wrapper, and didn't turn on the light. "Ssh, Ada Jane, you will wake the *dead*!" Her voice was a fierce whisper, and Ada knew it was her father Mama was worried about, not the dead. If Daddy didn't sleep, he took it out on her mother the next morning, and the bad mood might even continue when he got home from the

3

mill. Mostly, he barked at her, but Ada worried that someday he'd outright hit her.

Mama sank onto the edge of the bed and swept the damp hair off Ada's face. She never stayed mad for long. "Bad dream?"

"I was being kind of hunted. By real scary men. And there were dead children."

"My goodness, honey, what on earth brought *that* on?"

At her mama's light touch, Ada's heart settled back into its regular rhythm. "I don't know," she lied.

"You weren't up reading again, were you? One of those mystery stories you like so much?"

"No, ma'am."

"Well, you go back to sleep now. Think about something sweet, like the apple pie I'm aiming to make tomorrow."

But the shadows that flitted across her room resembled branches of a tree, and Ada was awake for much of the night.

§ § §

The head librarian, Miss Ruthie, could be harsh at times, physically removing girls from the main reading room for giggling, grabbing boys' arms with unexpected strength if they dashed past her circulation desk. She was a woman of considerable size, older than Ada's parents, and had acquired the nickname "Mad Old Maid" from young people who had incurred her wrath.

But if she took to a child, the way she had to Ada at an early age, Miss Ruthie was a guardian angel. She introduced Ada to the wonders of authors like Charlotte Brontë and Pearl Buck, and showed her photos of breathtaking places Miss Ruthie herself had visited with her friend, Miss Cicely, like the Grand Canyon and the Everglades. The librarian also had an uncanny knowledge of just about everything that had ever happened in North Carolina, right on back to colonial days, so Ada was certain she would be able to tell her something about the postcard.

Figuring out how to approach Miss Ruthie without admitting where the souvenir came from, however, was a puzzle. Still, the more days that went by with the photo in Ada's possession, the worse it would be for her if she were caught. On a quiet afternoon in the library, Ada waited until Miss Ruthie's break. The librarian always took fifteen minutes late in the day, disappearing behind a door with a frosted glass window marked OFFICE.

Ada approached the door and rapped on it gently, once. When there was no answer, she repeated the knock more forcefully.

Miss Ruthie answered with a dour look reserved for children who didn't appreciate the sacredness of the public library. Wisps of smoke drifted in the air behind her.

"*Yes*, Ada?"

It wasn't the friendly, melodic *Yes, Ada?* she was accustomed to when Miss Ruthie took her questions. Ada was sorry she had ventured this far, but it was too late to do an about-face.

"I wanted to show you something," she said.

"I am on my break, Ada. Can't it wait?"

"It's . . . not something I can show you out *here*," she explained.

Miss Ruthie waved her in and nodded for her to sit, but there wasn't a single chair that was not covered in books and magazines. The librarian stubbed out her unfinished cigarette, and tossed a pack of Chesterfields into a desk drawer.

"You did *not* see me smoking," she instructed with a sly smile, as she sat down behind her desk. "Well, don't just stand there, child. What's so important?"

Ada opened her school bag and fished through her papers until her fingers reached the cardboard of the postcard, which she laid on the desk. "Do you know what this is?"

Miss Ruthie's face went gray, like she might be sick. She flipped the postcard upside down on her blotter.

"Where did you get this, Ada?"

"I found it . . . somewhere."

The librarian bit her upper lip, and Ada's heart beat double-time. Miss Ruthie might press her further, but if Ada were lucky she would let the word *somewhere* lie between them like a dead dog no one wanted to touch.

"I see," the librarian said, and Ada's pulse slowed. Miss Ruthie adjusted her glasses to read the inscription on the back of the card. "You are surely old enough to know people are capable of great cruelty."

"Yes, ma'am."

"You know unspeakable things happened to the Jews during the war."

Ada nodded, not sure how that related to the colored men. She didn't exactly understand what had happened to the Jews, but she reckoned it was something bad. Her mother's youngest brother, Uncle Rad, had been involved in freeing people from camps and whispered on their back porch late one night about prisoners who "looked like skeletons."

"This incident . . ." Miss Ruthie began, then stopped and started again. "I was a girl not much older than you when this happened, but I never forgot it. The newspaper here was full of it."

Ada waited, seconds slipping away on a wall clock above Miss Ruthie's head.

"Somebody killed a white family in Salisbury. This was, oh, forty-some years ago. I don't recall their name now. Anyway, they were butchered with an ax, and their house was set on fire. Folks got it into their heads that their hired hands, three Negroes, were to blame. A mob found them guilty, and they were tortured and lynched, just like that." Miss Ruthie turned the photo right side up again. "Thousands of folks watched. Some came in from other counties. People took . . . pictures, like this, and made postcards out of them."

"Oh!" Ada said. Her stomach felt like it had been squeezed through her mama's wringer washer. Forty years ago her daddy was a little boy not even Foster's age, so he couldn't possibly have been involved in the lynching—but had he witnessed it? And who had given him such a gruesome souvenir?

Miss Ruthie's eyes seemed to focus on an ink spot on the blotter, just to the right of the postcard. "Did you get this from home?" The question was so unexpected that Ada had no choice but to nod yes.

"My daddy's from Salisbury," she said.

Miss Ruthie handed the postcard back, then removed her glasses to rub her eyes. "You best put this back where you found it, Ada," she said. "I doubt anybody meant for you to see it."

Ada slipped the card back into her bag and left the office. She took a volume of the encyclopedia to an empty table in the main reading room and pretended to read it. Miss Ruthie didn't come out as expected at 3:30. She was a full six minutes late.

§ § §

Ada replaced the postcard two days later, when her daddy was at work and her mother was peeling potatoes. She didn't need to look at it again after her talk with Miss Ruthie, because the image was branded in her mind.

She was settling the envelope back into its secret place, relieved she hadn't been caught, when her mother's voice behind her, sharp as a paring knife, made her jump.

"Ada Jane! What are you doing?" Jane Shook was not a tall woman, but she towered in the doorframe, hands on her hips, face red and pinched. "You come here."

Except for the occasional swat on the behind, her mama never hit her, but she had a strong grip that left its mark on tender arms. Her fingers wrapped so tightly around Ada's forearm it felt like she might faint.

"What are you doing, snooping around in here?" she asked, squeezing harder for emphasis. "You got something to say for yourself?"

"No, ma'am," Ada replied, tears filling the corners of her eyes. "Please, mama."

"'Please, mama,' what?"

"Please, *please*, don't tell him."

Her mama's grip relaxed and changed to light strokes, as if she could erase the pain she'd inflicted. "Your daddy has private things," she said. "You best respect that."

"Yes, ma'am."

7

"And you stay out of this shed. It's no place for a girl."

Ada's head bobbed up and down, then she broke free and tore off toward the house. From the kitchen window, she watched for her mother to emerge from the shed, but it took longer than Ada expected for her to close the door and return to her chores. That evening, Ada waited for a fight between her parents that never came. The house was oddly silent, almost like nobody lived there.

Madam Librarian

1957

Her predecessor, Miss Gladdie Johnston, had left a handwritten checklist so the new librarian wouldn't neglect any tasks, and by 7:50 a.m. on the first day of school, Ada had accomplished each one, in order. The newspapers were on display, the encyclopedia volumes alphabetical, the books neatly shelved, the card catalog drawers flush with the cabinet, the oak tables set with eight chairs each. Ada ran a finger over a carving on one of the tables—"JB + FT" with a pierced heart—wondering how long ago the student had left the mark.

Giving a final pat to her bun, Ada swung open the library door. A barrage of epithets immediately met her ears—ugly words she had heard plenty of times in her twenty-two years but had never herself uttered.

Principal Norris had given the faculty and staff a briefing about integration during in-service day the previous week, and admitted he did not know what level of resistance they would face. "Superintendent Garinger says this is the right thing to do. Those were his exact words," the principal announced.

Just down the hall from the library, the building's front doors were wide open, and Principal Norris was ushering Mary Burney, the school's first enrolled Negro student, into the building. Hostile white students and adults had created a human barrier across the entrance. A few boys spat on the ground in front of the girl and the principal as they attempted to pass. On the sidelines, photographers from the local papers snapped rounds of shots, while reporters scribbled in notebooks. Two police officers stood at attention on either side of the door with poker faces.

Mr. Norris shoved the throng aside and steered Mary through the doors with one hand on her left shoulder. Then he turned and spoke to the crowd at the top of his voice: "Students, report to your classrooms immediately! This is a school, not a circus tent. The rest of you, I will call on the help of these officers if you don't disperse."

Ada stood in the library doorframe, half in, half out of the hallway, where more students and some faculty members had gathered to witness the event. Mary was petite for an eighth-grader and could have easily passed for eleven or twelve. Her tailored blouse and full skirt were meticulously pressed, her straightened hair held back with a stiff plastic headband. Ada couldn't tell from the girl's impassive face how she felt about being plunged into the fracas. She had read in the paper that Mary's father, a local civil rights activist, petitioned for her trans-fer to Central Charlotte Junior High on the grounds that it was more academically rigorous than the all-Negro school she had been attending, and that Mary's ambition was to go to college.

Ada felt like she was onstage in a play but had forgotten her lines. She took a step toward Mary, thinking she could improvise: *I'm new here, too*. But Ada was neither a Negress nor a transfer student, so the gesture seemed silly to her and she inched back.

A statuesque young woman not much older than Ada came forward at that moment and extended a hand to Mary. With her blonde bob and printed neck scarf, she had the casual look of someone who'd just gotten off a horse. She reminded Ada of the girls she'd attended college with in Chapel Hill.

"Mary, I am so pleased to make your acquaintance," she said. "I'm Miss Lively, and you are in my homeroom and also my second-period English class. Won't you please come with me?" The principal handed Mary off to the aptly named Miss Lively, who glanced unexpectedly toward Ada and nodded recognition.

Back inside her domain, Ada could feel her heart doing double time. She hadn't realized integration by a single student would entail such ugliness. The white folks she knew were all decent people; why would anybody torment such a little girl? But when it came right down to it, Ada had little in the way of real life experience. Principal Norris had guessed as much, but took a chance on hiring her anyway.

"What makes you think you can handle this job?" he had asked at her interview. "Your only experience seems to be as a library assistant while you were at Carolina."

"I am passionate about helping young people discover books and develop their mental ability," she said immediately—a statement she'd rehearsed, but which she believed to her bones. It was what she had learned at the feet of Miss Ruthie.

"Negroes, too?" the principal pressed.

The question caught her off guard. She knew integration was likely to start—it had been a full three years since the *Brown* decision, and the city couldn't hold off much longer—but the schools enrolling students were still unannounced when she interviewed for jobs. Principal Norris was the only one to suggest Central might be among the test cases.

Ada's voice sounded tinny in her own ears. "Yes, sir, absolutely," she answered. "My mentor, Miss Ruth Mitford . . . maybe you have heard of her? She was fired from her job as a public librarian right here in Charlotte for supporting Negro literature of a pro-integration slant. Back in 1950."

"I remember that incident." Mr. Norris looked like he had taken a bite of something sour. "Miss Shook, the school librarian need not be an activist. In fact, it's better not to be. You just need to serve all the children."

Aside from Miss Ruthie's influence, nothing in Ada's background had prepared her to serve Negro students as well as white, and she doubted she was alone in that among the faculty members. She had grown up in a segregated cotton mill community, been educated in whites-only schools, ridden on buses with demarcation lines for Colored Passengers. She still attended a church whose pews were bursting with people who looked just like her. Her daddy, who had grown up poor on a farm, still sometimes used the word *nigger*, although her mother called him out when he did. His souvenir postcard of a lynching was still seared in her brain. It was something no one in her family had ever acknowledged or discussed.

"Folks have to want to change, that's the long and short of it," Miss Ruthie had said as she was packing up thirty years of belongings to leave the public library for good. "We Southerners are just too headstrong to acknowledge our sorry history for what it is."

At the time, Ada hadn't really understood Miss Ruthie's meaning, or her choice of words. Why *We*? Why *our*? Now it felt like change with a capital *C* had come and occupied a seat at Central.

§ § §

Ada was scheduled to supervise the first cafeteria period with the assistant principal, but when she was in the hallway she could not quite remember which way to go. She stood staring dumbly at her feet, as if they might instinctively find the way, when she heard whistling behind her, a tune she couldn't place. Except for hymns, Ada could not keep music or lyrics in her head. She glanced back and saw Miss Lively, walking toward her with a smile that suggested trouble.

If it had been a man whistling and smiling mischievously, she might have thought it fresh. She'd had plenty of experiences in college with boys who whistled at her, stared her up and down, or even touched her like they had bought the right. There had also been the distasteful matter of the professor who taught cataloging. He was a married man with at least three young children, but that hadn't stopped him from stroking Ada's hair during a visit to his office when all she had come for was clarification about her final project. "Such a lovely color," he had said, letting some strands fall through his fingers. "Not brown and not red. Russet, I think."

Ada forced herself to come up with a friendly remark for Miss Lively. Sometimes people mistook her shyness for being snobby and aloof, and her goal in her new job was to be liked as well as respected. "That sure is a catchy tune," was all she could muster on the spot.

"Do you know it?" Closer up, Miss Lively was even taller than she had looked at a distance. In loafers, she towered a good six inches over Ada in her smart heels.

"Popular music is not my forte."

"What *is* your forte?" Miss Lively asked with one slightly raised eyebrow.

"Books, I guess," Ada said. She never really thought of herself as having a particular skill. She was certainly not the quick mind and passionate observer of life Miss Ruthie had been.

"That makes perfect sense for the school librarian. You *are* Miss Shook, aren't you? I noticed you on in-service day and again in the hallway this morning. I must say, you're a big improvement over that old fossil, Miss Gladdie. I thought the woman would never retire!"

"And you're Miss Lively." She forced herself to say what she was really thinking and not just what was polite. "I . . . truly admired how you took charge of the . . . situation this morning."

Miss Lively's smile spread across her cheeks. "Call me Cam," she said, reaching out a hand browned by the sun. Ada's looked small in hers, as if Cam could snap it like the bones of a finch. "English and girls' basketball."

"That explains why you're so tall!" Ada knew the second she spoke that it was impolite to call attention to someone's unusual height. She felt her cheeks flush, but Cam swooped in for the save.

"Yes, indeed. My daddy stretched me out on a rack when I was little so I'd be the absolute best height for coaching hoops."

Ada laughed again. These quips reminded her of the finest days at college, when she was most at ease in her own skin. Now living back home with her parents, she missed her best friend, Natalie, who was with her new husband at Fort Bragg. The pain of Natalie's absence was an actual ache sometimes, like part of her had been cut out. Ada had never admitted that to anybody, because she knew she wasn't supposed to feel so strongly about another girl.

"You'll excuse me, Miss Lively, but I have cafeteria duty in—" with a glance at her Timex "—seven minutes, and I am not even sure I remember where it is."

"Down the stairs to the left," Cam said. "Just follow the unpleasant smells. This is my third year, and I have yet to eat there."

"I guess we'll be seeing each other again soon." *Explain yourself, you fool*, Ada thought. "I mean, you being the English teacher."

"I shall require your services before you know it," Cam said. Was something in her eye, or did she actually wink? "Oh, and by the way, the song is called 'Marian the Librarian.' I'll have to sing you the lyrics sometime." When Ada looked blank, Cam added, "From *The Music Man*? It's about a man trying to woo a librarian, but the joke is he can't talk to her in the library."

"Oh!" Ada said, surprised that someone had taken the time to write a song about a librarian. "Yes, I would very much like to hear that."

§ § §

Ada's first week was a haze of cataloging, placing book orders, checking out and re-shelving books, and answering requests from teachers for an introduction to the library for their students. The two ladies who had been volunteers under Miss Gladdie made it clear they knew more than Ada about running a school library. "Let me show you how Miss Gladdie did it, dear," the one named Mrs. Pierce said.

On top of the work, there were calls from reporters sniffing around for a faculty or staff member to comment on Mary Burney's enrollment. As instructed, Ada referred them to Principal Norris. The faculty lounge was abuzz all week about the "situation" of integration—both locally and in faraway Little Rock, Arkansas, where the National Guard had been brought in to protect the nine Negro students. The chatter gave the lounge the feel of a bunker. Ada deduced from overheard snippets that a number of incidents had taken place involving Mary and other students. Cam Lively had apparently broken up some intimidating pushing during second lunch period on opening day and told everyone she was keeping track of infractions against Mary.

"Should get herself a job with the NAACP, if you ask me," Ada heard a teacher complain to a colleague.

At home, too, Ada couldn't get away from the issue. "So they let that colored girl in?" her father asked at supper after her first day. Her curt reply of "It's the law, Daddy" was met with a rant about federal judges sticking their noses into folks' business. He had already made clear that he would pull Ada's younger brother, Foster, out of any school that enrolled colored students.

When Saturday rolled around, Ada wanted nothing more than to lose herself in a movie, with a bag of popcorn she didn't have to share. The afternoon was temperate and dry, so she walked to the Plaza Theater, close to a two-mile hike and the most exercise she'd had all week, if she didn't count trekking up and down the school stairs for cafeteria duty.

At the movies, she picked her spot carefully, six seats in from the aisle and toward the back (but not so far back as to be sitting close to any lovebirds). She settled down in the dark with her popcorn and the Coming Attractions, savoring the prospect of the meaty drama *The Three Faces of Eve*. But then two women entered the theater noisily and plopped down in the row in front of her, partially blocking her view when they leaned their heads into each other to whisper back and forth. She wanted to ask them to be quiet and considerate of others—and to keep their heads apart, for goodness' sake—when the one woman's distinctive blonde bob caught her attention.

Should she say hello to Cam and risk being asked to join them, when she had so looked forward to watching the movie alone? And if she said nothing and Cam turned around, would she get the reputation of being a stuck-up so-and-so?

You can do it, Natalie would have coaxed. She was naturally outgoing and always tried to urge Ada out of her shell. *Just tap her on the shoulder and say hello.*

But Natalie wasn't there, so Ada quietly moved herself and her popcorn back several rows. It was farther from the screen than she liked, and uncomfortably close to a bobby-soxer and her attentive crew-cut boyfriend, but she felt she had dodged a potentially sticky situation.

Her decision carried a price tag. She couldn't focus on the movie because her eyes kept traveling away from Joanne Woodward and Lee J. Cobb and toward Cam and her companion, especially when their heads almost touched. *They must be fast friends,* Ada thought, as she and Nat had been. Ada and Nat had eaten most of their meals together, taken many of the same classes, gone to mixers where they talked to no one but each other. Some people thought they were sisters, they were that close, but with Natalie's porcelain skin and coal-black hair, there wasn't even a faint resemblance.

"That was one dumb movie," the crew-cut boy remarked as the credits rolled. Ada considered dashing out of the theater before the lights went up, but instead she forced herself to stay put and try to catch Cam's eye. Cam's head was bent as she walked down the aisle listening to her friend. *They're discussing the movie already,* Ada thought with a pang of jealousy. *They're going for coffee now to hash it all out.* Which was exactly what she and Natalie would have done. Ada didn't interrupt them, but instead sneaked out of the theater as soon as she could and caught a bus home, where she began her weekly missive to Natalie:

Dearest Nat, what a whirlwind week for yours truly!

§ § §

"And which of Eve's faces did you like the best, Miss Shook? Eve White or Eve Black? Or maybe the sweet Jane?"

The voice behind her in the faculty lunchroom sounded as if it might be making fun of her. But when Ada turned and met Cam Lively's eyes, she knew she had read something into her tone that wasn't there. Cam's head was tilted, waiting for Ada's answer with a look of genuine interest.

"That was you at the Plaza on Saturday, wasn't it?" Cam asked. "I caught you out of the corner of my eye, but you'd vanished by the time I said to my friend 'I know that girl!'"

"Oh, you were there, too?" Ada said, as innocently as she could muster.

"I made the mistake of bringing my college friend Lu, and she was positively horrified by the whole thing. She kept whispering all through the show, 'What in the world did you bring me to?' She's as close to me as a sister, but sometimes I wonder why! I was going to invite you to come along for coffee. I was hoping the two of us could enlighten her. But no such luck."

Ada smiled shyly at the words *the two of us*, and at her own incorrect assessment that Cam and the other woman were best friends.

"So what did you think?"

"I thought Joanne Woodward was perfect," Ada said, deeming that a safe conclusion to draw about an acclaimed performance. "The movie adhered pretty close, um, closely to the book. Except they did make the two doctors who treated her into one man. I guess that was just easier."

"You must have an eclectic taste in books," Cam observed.

Ada didn't explain she had borrowed it from the library and returned it unfinished. She thought she might seem more worldly and mysterious if she just nodded vaguely, and less like the scholarship girl who still occasionally struggled with grammar.

"Do you go to the movies much?" Cam asked.

"Every chance I get."

"Well, we will have to go together some time. I love the movies and absolutely hate to go alone. There's no one to talk to about it after it's over."

Ada nodded, unable to think of anything to reply but "Yes, let's do that." She left it purposely open, aware that she was both drawn to Cam and scared of the possibility of her friendship at the same time.

17

The following Thursday, Cam brought her eighth-grade English students for library class. Ada had practiced her presentation several times; it had earned her an A+ at Carolina from a favorite professor who called it "strong and informative, yet accessible." But delivering it in the mirror at home was different from standing in front of twenty young faces—and Cam.

The students filed into the library for second period. Mary Burney was next to last into the room, her eyes scanning for a spot. She took a place at the table farthest from the front of the room, where only two other students sat.

"There's a seat up here, if you'd like," Ada offered, but Mary plunked her books down in the back anyway. Cam sat next to Mary with an encouraging smile on her face, but instead of being put at ease, Ada felt a rush of intimidation.

"Now please pay attention to Miss Shook," Cam said. "She's going to divulge secrets that will help y'all this term. And there just might be a quiz."

Pencils were poised for taking notes, but when Ada opened her mouth to speak, no sound came out. Some of the students looked puzzled, others snickered. Cam chided them softly, but she herself seemed bemused. Ada whispered, "Excuse me," took a sip of lukewarm tea from her cup, and started over. This time her voice shuddered through several sentences before finally arriving full force. While the presentation had taken a full forty minutes when she rehearsed it, there were still twenty minutes on the clock when she raced to her conclusion. She stood staring at the unsympathetic faces, willing them to disappear.

"Well, that was right informative, wasn't it," Cam said. "I think I learned some things myself." She prodded them for questions, but the room remained silent. "Well, let's say 'Thank you, Miss Shook' and get out of her hair."

"Thank you, Miss Shook," echoed through the room.

Cam waited as they filed back into the hallway one by one.

"Thanks for your time," she called to Ada, with a smile that seemed forced and held none of its previous sparkle.

She knows I am duller than dirt, Ada thought. "I am so sorry," she said quickly, before Cam could leave and snip off their friendship in the bud. She actually reached out and touched the sleeve of Cam's linen blouse—the sleeve! Cam's eyes traveled to the spot Ada's fingers had brushed.

And then Ada let the truth erupt out of her. "I have this frightful fear of public speaking. It dates back to having to recite Timrod's 'Ode to the Confederate Dead' in fourth grade. After that, the boys all called me 'Ada Sh-sh-oo-oo-k.'"

Cam laughed, her head snapping back with genuine delight. "Well, that experience would be enough to traumatize anybody," she replied. "Don't worry, you did fine. Nice and succinct. Miss Gladdie would've droned on and on till we were all catatonic. The glassier our eyes, the better."

At the door, Cam glanced back over her shoulder. "How about a movie this Saturday?" she asked. "You seen *Band of Angels* yet?"

She shook her head, afraid to speak and spoil everything again. She had avoided that particular movie because Natalie had written to her that it was "no *Gone with the Wind,* that's for sure!"

"I'm warning you, though, I might insist you recite the odious 'Ode,'" Cam said. "Just for fun." Ada heard her soft whistle again as the door closed behind her.

§ § §

Natalie had been right: the movie was no *Gone with the Wind.* Clark Gable played a Southern gentleman once again, but he looked drained and old. All the girls she knew, including Natalie, considered Rhett Butler the embodiment of sex appeal. "My goodness, the way he carried Scarlett up those stairs!" Natalie had practically drooled when they saw the re-release of the movie together in college. But to Ada, Rhett's threat to snap Scarlett's neck with his bare hands was just menacing.

"I bet you've read *this* book, too," Cam had said when they met in the lobby of the theater to buy popcorn. Ada admitted she had, and that reading was her great escape. "'A good book can carry you into a different world,' that's what a dear librarian told me when I was a girl. She said reading is like being on a wonderful trip, or engaging in a conversation with the writer."

"A conversation. I never thought of it that way. I like it." Although Ada had her change purse ready, Cam waved her off and paid for both bags of popcorn. "My treat. You're the new girl. So tell me about the 'dear librarian.' Did she inspire your career?"

No one had ever asked her that before, and she was glad for the shift in topic. Ada had been inwardly struggling with how to tell Cam that the "conversation" with Robert Penn Warren, author of *Band of Angels*, had confused her, and that she had closed the cover on his novel unsure what he thought or wanted *her* to think. At times, it conformed to what Ada had learned in school—that benevolent planters treated slaves like family, and that slavery was not as bad as bleeding hearts made out. But Warren portrayed as many evil planters as kind, and the Yankees in the novel were, for the most part, unredeemable interlopers. Who were the villains and who were the good guys?

The movie, it turned out, was just as baffling. Ada spent most of it aware that Cam was sitting right next to her, formulating an opinion of the movie, and that she would be expected to share her own thoughts after. With Natalie, that had always felt natural, because she knew her friend wouldn't judge her. In retrospect, though, they had never discussed anything too political or that brought their very upbringing into question. And Ada would have never commented on how lovely a particular actress was—she knew she was only supposed to notice and appreciate the men.

When they exited the theater and Cam asked the inevitable "What did you think?," Ada picked through her thoughts cautiously. "Well, they sure truncated the story," she replied as they strolled down the street toward a coffee shop. "In the book, Manty has a full life after Hamish. She gets married and everything."

"Interesting," Cam said, but she said she hadn't read the novel, so the conversation stumbled. "You know, Warren started out pro-segregation, one of the Southern Agrarians. He made a public shift after the *Brown* decision, even published a piece in *Life* about the South searching for its soul. He interviewed everybody from the NAACP right down to citizens' council folks."

Ada felt embarrassed not to know this, but her final year in college had been a blur as she struggled to finish the requirements for her library science degree before her scholarship money ran out. "I seem to have missed that particular issue," she said.

"I was glad to see one of our venerable Southern writers making the shift. But I still think Lillian Smith is the one to read on the topic of segregation. You know Lillian Smith? Author of *Strange Fruit?* Now that would make *some* movie! No benevolent planters or happy darkies singing spirituals on the riverbank!"

Ada nodded, but once again had nothing to add. "I have heard of Miss Smith, of course," she said, "but I haven't read her work."

"Aha! Something I've read that Madam Librarian hasn't! You'd like her, I think. She's a truly independent woman. Never married. She wrote a nonfiction book that I highly recommend—*Killers of the Dream.* She talks about how fiercely folks will hold onto something they just take for granted. Like segregation."

Cam seemed bent on discussing politics, and Ada badly wanted to get back to something that felt more comfortable to her, like books. Once when she had admired Nat's conversational skills, Nat had told her she could turn around any dialogue with modesty or a little joke at her own expense. "This will sound funny," Ada said now to Cam, with what she hoped was a self-deprecating laugh, "but I'm afraid I don't have a real strong opinion about that."

They hesitated on the threshold of the coffee shop, the awkwardness of the moment overtaking them. Cam had been about to reach for the door handle, but her hand went down to her side instead. Her face was tight as a rubber band stretched to its limit.

"Now I know you are a smart girl," Cam said, lowering her voice as if to keep it under control. "You don't seem like a fiddledee-dee kind of girl to me. My mother saddled me with the name Camellia, and I grew up around belles. But you? You have read Robert Penn Warren, for God's sake. You live in Dixie in this day and age, you are a librarian, and yet you don't have an opinion on segregation? I don't find that funny, Ada, I find it damn sad."

The swearing made her flinch, and Ada drew back a little, holding her pocketbook in front of her like a shield. Disparate thoughts about segregation tumbled in her head. She knew it was wrong to treat Negroes differently, but there was the question of states' rights being violated by the Supreme Court ruling—at least, that was her daddy's view. Her pastor had preached against integration more than once, and the evils that could come from "mixing the races." Miss Ruthie, though, had encouraged her to see things through more than one lens: *Be an independent thinker, Ada.* Miss Ruthie, she suspected, would have told her to ask if she could borrow the Lillian Smith book from Cam.

But before Ada could suggest that, Cam blurted out, "You know, I made a mistake. I forgot I have to be somewhere at four. I'll have to take a rain check on coffee. I guess I'll see you next week."

Ada was left standing in front of the coffee shop still clutching her purse and wondering how an afternoon she had looked forward to had turned out so wrong.

§ § §

On Monday, Ada was getting ready to take lunch and leave the library in Mrs. Pierce's hands. She was hoping to run into Cam in the faculty lounge so she could tell her she'd been thinking all weekend about what she'd said about segregation. But her plans changed when, from the window of the library, Ada witnessed the attack unfold.

Mary Burney was sitting on one of the low brick walls surrounding the schoolyard, her books and notebooks stacked next

22

to her. She looked the way she always did, isolated and stoic. In the two weeks since classes had begun, Ada had never once seen her with anyone, not in the hallways, not at recess or in the library.

Ada had spoken to Mary only once, when the girl seemed to need help finding a book. Principal Norris had said she was a straight-A student, with a reading level far above her grade level. Maybe Ada could steer her toward choices like *A Tree Grows in Brooklyn* or *The Diary of Anne Frank*.

"You like novels?" Ada had asked when she found Mary staring into the stacks of fiction as if she didn't know where to begin.

"Yes, ma'am." Mary ran a finger tentatively over a few spines.

"There's a lot to pick from," Ada said. "If you'd like a recommendation, I'm happy to assist. What appeals to you?"

"My daddy said I should just start at the A's and work my way through," Mary replied, closing down the exchange.

"Well, that's good advice," Ada said, not one to come between a girl and her father, although she would have put more thought to Mary's interests. When Mary was checking out, Ada saw that she had indeed gone the alphabetical route and selected Louisa May Alcott's *Little Women*.

"Excellent choice," Ada said, and Mary allowed herself to smile.

Now, in the schoolyard, Mary was reading, possibly the very book she'd borrowed, when a white boy strode up to her, cocky and self-assured. Ada knew he was a seventh-grader named Virgil Chance; she'd had to issue him a detention slip one afternoon for disrupting the library. Like Mary, he was small for his age, and probably fodder for older bullies. His words were indistinct through the open windows, but *snarling* described the expression on his face. Two equally angry-looking boys stood behind him. Virgil poked Mary's shoulder, and she turned herself and her book away, as if to ignore him, which only served to rile him more. He poked her other shoulder, and Mary gathered up her belongings to leave. At that moment, Virgil leaned forward and directed a wad of spit onto the front of Mary's crisp white blouse, while the boys behind him whooped with laughter. Mary stood up, and Virgil pushed her a third time, even more forcefully, until she fell backward into a hawthorn bush.

"Eeny, meeny, miney, mo, catch a nigger by the toe!" The common children's rhyme soared through the windows.

"Go away!" Mary shrieked, then muttered something Ada couldn't hear.

Ada scanned the yard for the teachers on duty. But although Miss Kilwin and Mrs. Lamott's heads turned, they made no move in Mary's direction. Ada had overheard Miss Kilwin grumbling in the faculty lounge: "Well, why would they want to go to a school where they aren't welcome?"

Ada's first thought was to run across the hall and ask for Cam's help. Cam would leave her class, walk onto the schoolyard with the authority she commanded, and haul that boy's behind down to the principal's office. She wouldn't act self-righteous about it; she would simply *act*.

But there was no time to engage Cam. A few more children, girls and boys, had joined the original three, and a circle was forming around Mary. Each time the girl tried to free herself, a hand came out to push her back. And still, the teachers in the yard seemed unconcerned. Mrs. Kilwin actually consulted her wristwatch, as if willing recess to end.

Ada left the library without a word to Mrs. Pierce and almost tripped down the side steps to the schoolyard. She parted the circle of students roughly. Despite their intimidating manner, they were still just children, and it was surprisingly easy to yank Virgil by his skinny arm. "Ow!" he moaned. "You're hurting me, lady!"

"You will address me as Miss Shook," she said in a voice that came out so strong it surprised her. As she dragged him toward the building, she glanced back and saw Mrs. Lamott approach the students, who were already dispersing without their ringleader. "All right, that's enough of *that*!" the teacher said, clapping her hands.

Principal Norris was in conversation with a mother in the

reception area adjoining his office when Ada arrived with Virgil, who squealed like a stuck pig.

"Is there a problem, Miss Shook?"

"This boy spit on Mary Burney," Ada replied, releasing her grip on Virgil's arm. "He *spit* on her."

"Called me 'white trash,'" Virgil hissed.

"I saw you start it, Virgil," Ada said. "Don't tell fibs."

"Well, now," the principal said. "Virgil, have a seat in there." He motioned toward the open door of his office, and Virgil shuffled through it.

"Miss Shook," Principal Norris began. "You remember your interview for this job?"

"Very well, sir."

"I told you that a school librarian should not be an activist."

The principal's words made Ada's face hot. She was being called out, and in front of a parent. Even Virgil could probably hear the dressing-down through the open office door. "I don't understand," she said, lowering her voice. "You told me to serve *all* the students."

"Including young Mr. Chance," the principal said. "We can't have students calling each other names, now can we?" He pulled out a handkerchief and dabbed at his brow. "I will handle this from here, Miss Shook. But thank you for bringing the matter to my attention."

Why is using the term white trash *name-calling, but* nigger *is not?* Ada wanted to ask. But Principal Norris slammed his office door behind him, leaving her standing there like an errant child.

Back in the library, Ada did the unthinkable—she asked the three students who were studying to leave, told Mrs. Pierce she was no longer needed that day, and then locked the door from the inside. She collapsed into her desk chair, overwhelmed with sobs so violent she didn't hear the first knocks at the door. The rattling of the doorknob and the sound of Cam's voice, low and insistent, finally got her attention. "Ada, it's me—Cam. Open up. Please."

Ada dabbed at her eyes with her handkerchief, leaving dots of mascara behind on the printed cotton. She blew her nose, then unlocked the door.

A few other teachers, including Mrs. Lamott, had gathered behind Cam in the hallway, poking their heads around to get a better look at Ada's distress. ". . . locked the door!" she heard Mrs. Pierce say. "Can you imagine!" Cam slipped in and shut the rest of the hallway out.

"Cam, I . . ." Ada started but couldn't finish.

"I know, darlin'. It's all over school." The endearment, which no one had ever called her except men being too familiar, sent a chill up Ada's arms.

"I should have gotten Mary out of there instead," Ada said. "I did it all wrong."

"You did it just fine. Mary is shook up, but she is a strong girl. Norris is going to send her home. Though I'm not sure what good that will do. It's that little no-'count redneck who should be sent home—on suspension."

"I don't understand what happened in the office. I actually thought he was mad at *me*."

"Norris is a Southern-fried hypocrite," Cam said. "I'm sure you know a million folks just like him, polite as Sunday on the out-side and bigoted as all get-out on the inside." Cam looped a strong arm around Ada's shoulders. The intimate gesture took her as much by surprise as the word *darlin'*, and she stiffened. She had cuddled up to Natalie on occasion, but this felt different. Ada could smell Cam's fragrance, something with the light aroma of oranges.

"Hey, can you believe it?" Cam said. "We are talking *out loud* in the library—in the middle of the school day!" She startled Ada again by launching into the song she had whistled on the first day of school: "'But what can I do in here/To catch your ear/I love you madly madly, Madam Librarian . . . Marian.'"

It was not a song for a woman to sing to another woman, but Cam performed it lightheartedly, like the friend Ada needed. She actually found herself laughing as Cam fumbled the words and substituted a lot of *da-dum, da-dum, da-dum, da-dum*s. Within a few minutes, Ada had blown her nose one last time and reopened the library door.

§ § §

By the end of the week, Mary had withdrawn from Central. As her homeroom teacher, Cam got the news early and told Ada. The daily paper carried the story, which quoted Mary's father.

"The principal told us he could not protect our daughter from further incidents," Theo Burney stated. "So after much thought, Mrs. Burney, Mary and I have made the difficult decision to change schools before more time goes by. Central is not an atmosphere conducive to Mary's learning." For the rest of the school year, he said, Mary would live with her mother's aunt "up north" and attend an integrated academy.

Mr. Norris made no official announcement, and soon Mary was just an anecdote, an interruption in an otherwise orderly school year. "He told me it was best not to make 'a fuss,'" Cam said. "You can bet he's breathing a sigh of relief. But if he thinks integration is over at this school or in this city, he'd best think again."

That was how Ada and Cam began having coffee together most days after school, their time together so crammed with conversation that it sometimes even spilled over into an early supper. They talked shop, of course, and current events, but Cam also taught Ada about sports while she kept Cam abreast of all the latest books she'd read reviews of. It was the best part of the day for Ada, though she still had no word for it but "friendship."

"You'll get a reputation, hanging out with me," Cam warned her, only half-joking.

But it wasn't Cam who had tainted how other faculty members saw her; her own response to Virgil Chance had done that. "Looks like we got us another one," Ada heard a faculty member whisper one day as she left the faculty lounge.

As the weather cooled and leaves crackled beneath her feet, Ada's thoughts still turned to Mary. Was she adjusting to her new surroundings? Had she made friends? Would she ever attend school in Charlotte again? The girl's features blurred in Ada's memory, but she still held a clear picture of her stoic demeanor.

In late October, a package addressed to *School Librarian* arrived at Central. Inside was the school's copy of *Little Women* wrapped in tissue, accompanied by a note written on ivory stationery. A one-dollar bill was tucked inside. *My daughter forgot to return this book before she left Central,* read the note. *She didn't mean to, and she is very sorry. I have enclosed a dollar to cover overdue fines. Thank you for understanding. Sincerely, Mrs. Theo Burney, Charlotte, North Carolina.*

Ada had forgotten about the novel. The sleeve inside the book bore the stamped date when Mary had checked it out. From the circulation files, Ada dug out the matching card, which carried Mary's round, childish signature. Ada had commended her choice, and the gesture had made Mary smile.

Now the volume felt like an artifact—no longer just a library book, but proof that Mary had been there and that something had happened at the school. At the end of the day, Ada deposited it on the cart for re-shelving, and Mrs. Pierce put it back in place without knowing where it had come from or that it was very overdue.

Ada would tell Cam about it later. But in the meantime, she penned a note to Mrs. Burney, returning the dollar. She had to start it over twice, writing several lines and crossing them out, rewriting and crossing them out again, until she was left with a single, unsatisfying sentence: *Please tell Mary I wish her all the best in wherever the future takes her. Yours truly, Ada Jane Shook, Librarian.*

The Book Club

1958

"Everybody calls me Lu," the woman in a pearl necklace and flowered sheath said. Ada recognized her immediately; she'd seen her at the movies with Cam.

Lu was dressed for a garden party, even though Cam had assured Ada the get-together at her apartment was "casual." Ada tugged at her simple pleated skirt, wishing she had worn her go-to-church dress instead.

As if she were the hostess, Lu poured Ada a cup of punch. "Cam asked me to make my famous Pink Paradise. You are in paradise after one sip!" The drink was fortified with something far stronger than Ada was accustomed to, and whatever rendered it pink seemed like an afterthought. Without any fanfare, Ada found a spot to abandon her cup behind a vase of daffodils, and popped a potato chip into her mouth to take away the bitter taste.

The second-story apartment hummed with the laughter of young women and a couple of men who obviously knew each other well but didn't get together often enough. At the center was Cam, who had begged Ada to come to the launch of her new book club.

"You will just love these folks," Cam said. Ada thought knowing a few more people outside of her job might be nice, and folks who read books and joined a club to talk about them were likely friends for a junior high school librarian. But really she had come for Cam. Over the course of a few months, they had become fast friends, meeting after school for coffee most days after Cam's basketball coaching.

At the book club, though, Cam left her to her own devices, and Ada felt a twinge of disappointment. She milled around the apartment, impressed that Cam had her own place, with two full bedrooms and a separate dining room—an apartment designed more for a small family than a single girl. Maybe she got help from her parents, Ada thought. Ada still lived at home, and it was hard to imagine managing rent on her salary. "You'll be married soon enough," her mother said when she got prickly about returning every evening to her tiny bedroom.

But she hadn't been on a single date with any of the men her mother and other church ladies introduced her to every Sunday. She kept waiting for marriage to interest her. "If you aren't careful, Ada Jane," a friend of her mother's commented, "men will get the wrong idea about you. They'll think you are a career girl." It wasn't the wrong idea at all. Ada had seen the lives of millworkers' wives up close and couldn't imagine relinquishing her hard-won education and position for their daily drudgery.

The tables and shelves of Cam's apartment were littered with framed photos—scenes of Cam at the beach, at a putt-putt range, at a wedding, a bar, another bar, always with friends, many of the same faces at the book club. In each shot, Cam's face filled with a big, easy-going grin as she draped an arm around someone's shoulders like it belonged there. She looked like happiness itself.

And then there were at least a dozen photos of her with a middle-aged man who had the same square jaw as Cam, the same deep-set eyes and effortless smile. They were on horses, in a park, next to a Christmas tree, in front of a sign that read *Davidson College*.

Cam appeared out of nowhere and tapped her shoulder, making Ada jump. "Sorry, darlin', I didn't mean to scare you." She placed a hand on the small of Ada's back, an intimate gesture Ada had only experienced with men who wanted something from her. When Cam did it, though, it just felt comfortable. "You getting to know people?"

"Some," Ada said. "I don't like to just barge in on conversations."

"Talk to Auggie," Cam suggested, pointing to a slender youth with a cowlick shooting up from his ginger hair. He looked like a teenager and reminded Ada a little of her younger brother, Foster. "He's one of my favorite people."

But Ada found small talk laborious, trying to think up things to say to strangers. To shift attention away from her poor social skills and keep Cam close by, she asked, "Is that your father in these photos?"

"Yes, ma'am. Thomas Jackson Lively—chair of English at Davidson College. Named for Stonewall, but he has spent his entire life decrying the Confederacy."

"You sure have a lot of photos of him."

"I don't!" A twinge of defensiveness crept into her voice, but then she laughed it off. "Well, I guess I do, if you start counting."

"You look like you get along right well."

"We do, most times. He can be pig-headed, but then folks have said that about me, too. How about you and your father? You get along?"

Ada took a deep breath while she considered how to answer. Her daddy had never gone past eighth grade and seemed to resent that his daughter won a scholarship to college. Ada was about to admit that to Cam when the woman named Lu turned up next to them. "You talking about T.J.?" she said. "Handsome devil, isn't he? I've always had a bit of a crush on him."

"Lu and I went to school together in Greensboro," Cam explained. "Woman's College, class of '54. Her folks live all the way over in Edenton, so she used to come home with me to Davidson some weekends."

"We were roommates two full years," Lu added. The coy way she said *roommates* made her even more of a mystery.

The mention of college launched Lu and Cam into a rapid-fire exchange of reminiscences ("Remember when you...?" "That is pure exaggeration, girl, and you know it!"), while Ada stood by like the proverbial third wheel. At a break in the small talk, she finally asked outright, "When do you think we'll start talking about the book?"

"You're the librarian, aren't you?" Lu said, as if nothing else could explain the desire to talk about a book at a book club.

"I am." Ada had taken time out of her regular reading schedule to fit in *The Grass Harp* by Truman Capote. She had jotted her mixed responses to the story in a leather notebook Natalie had given her for graduation. Ada used the notebook sparingly, saving each page for something important, and her preparation for the book club had taken up two full sheets. Having put that much effort into it, she was darned well going to discuss the book.

"Well, honey, most of us are just here to drink and gossip!"

"Deluth, please," Cam said, and placed a hand on her friend's forearm. "Let's let everyone refresh their drinks and then we'll start the discussion, how's that sound?"

It sounded fine to Ada, although she was wondering what kind of name "Deluth" was and what sort of discussion could possibly take place among folks who were there for other reasons entirely.

Indeed, when Cam announced that discussion was going to commence, some of the guests spilled out onto the front porch, which overlooked the oak-lined road. Gauzy curtains blew in the breeze, cutting the glare of the afternoon sun. "Not too loud, please," Cam admonished them. "Mind the neighbors."

Of those remaining in the living room, Lu and a girl named Shirley Ann admitted they hadn't gotten past the first few pages of the novel. Auggie, who was older than he seemed from across the room, had finished about half the volume, as had the young man named Twig who sat next to him, closer than men were supposed to. Some others had "almost" finished, and Cam said she had turned the last page just that morning. "I was busy grading papers," she said.

"That what they call it nowadays?" Lu asked.

"That's one of my lines," Auggie said.

"Behave yourselves, y'all," Cam replied. She turned to Ada, who sat across from her on a stiff dining-room chair. "Ada, you okay on that chair? There's room on the sofa next to Auggie."

"Yeah, you're just a little bitty thing," Auggie agreed, making more space. "Twig, scoot down."

Ada changed seats, her shoulder brushing Auggie, who smelled like a delicious sprig of mint.

"Ada, I truly apologize for my friends. I bet you read the whole book, and you're thinking we're all just a bunch of yahoos."

Ada opened her mouth to respond, but Lu cut in again. "I for one don't understand why you picked *this* book, Cam. Or maybe Ada chose it? Maybe if you'd picked something more interesting by the little sissy, I would've bothered to read it, like the one about the transvestite. What's that one called again?"

"I didn't pick anything," Ada said. "I'm not very familiar with Truman Capote."

"It's Capo-*tee*, dear," Lu corrected.

Ada had never heard anyone pronounce his name and could feel herself reddening right down to her chest.

"Lu, don't you need to get yourself a drink or something?" Twig asked.

"I picked the book," Cam said. "I thought you'd want to read something newer. And he didn't write a novel *about* a transvestite. It has a transvestite character, that's all."

"People say the ending means the main character is a homosexual," Lu said. "Now that would have been interesting reading, don't you think, Ada?"

"Oh," Ada said, startled to be singled out. "I couldn't say." She meant about the book, but it came out wrong, like a defense. In church, the lesson of Sodom and Gomorrah was one of the preacher's fallback sermons, and she had heard plenty of derogatory names for men who liked other men. But she had never been in casual company—and mixed company, at that—where someone spoke the word *homosexual* out loud.

"Why, honey, you are blushing," Lu said.

"Leave her alone," Auggie said. "You are always trying to stir up trouble. Don't pay her any mind, Ada."

Cam turned to Lu. "Since you haven't read the book, maybe you'd like to join the others on the porch."

33

"Aren't we touchy today," Lu said. "Aunt Flo must be visiting. I wasn't trying to hurt anybody. It just seemed obvious you didn't warn Ada."

The only sound was soft conversation from the direction of the porch.

"Warn me about what?"

"Why, about *us*, honey. About this very . . . *queer* assortment of folks."

Ada scanned the circle of faces. Auggie's was so close he seemed slightly distorted, like in a fun house. Even Cam, with whom she'd spent so many hours discussing books and work, looked unfamiliar. Ada's own face was burning, but she wasn't sure why. She smiled feebly, but the preacher's face as he raved about fire and brimstone kept popping into her mind.

"Will you excuse me a minute?" she said, making a move to get up. Auggie leaned over and whispered in her ear.

"Please don't leave. Miss Pardue is nothing but a trouble-maker," he said, attaching yet a third name to Lu.

"I just need to use the ladies'," she said. Cam offered to show her the way, but she waved her off, grabbed her pocketbook, and found the bathroom on her own.

Ada dabbed cool water on neck. In the mirror, she could read the fear in her look, the wide eyes that popped when she felt cornered, but she wasn't sure what there was to be afraid of. Except for Lu, they seemed like friendly, accommodating folks. She could get used to their light banter. Just spending time with Cam after school had made the words flow more easily out of her.

Ada's eyes took in the reflection of the room, the Carolina blue towels, the neat black and white tiles. At the sink, a white clamshell cradled a bar of Ivory soap. She knew she shouldn't, but she opened the medicine cabinet, where she found a women's razor, a half-used bottle of Bayer aspirin, and a tube of lipstick. In the six months she'd known her, Ada had never seen Cam wear any makeup at all. The shade, when she uncapped it, was a vivid coral, marked with someone's lip print. Ada wondered if it belonged to a woman in the book group, like Lu.

Cam had dropped plenty of hints about being an *independent* woman and a *free-thinker*, and she'd talked about admiring writers like Lillian Smith, who never married. Cam's talk hadn't scared Ada off. In fact, it intrigued her; it offered the possibility of an alternate life path. Even Miss Ruthie shared her home with a woman named Miss Cicely, and she did seem fulfilled.

Still, Ada hadn't really considered that women might keep their lipstick in the medicine cabinet for the next morning. The thought made her feel a little dizzy, and she closed the cabinet.

Auggie was waiting outside the bathroom door, leaning against the wall. "Sorry I took so long," she said, startled.

"I was waiting for you, hon," he said. "You looked a tad peaked." He took her hand and pulled her through a door that was slightly ajar. The curtains in the bedroom were drawn, and everything was in casual disarray. Auggie clicked his tongue as he shoved aside a copy of the Sunday paper from the rumpled bedclothes. "She's a secret slob," he said, "but we love her just the same. Here, come sit with me."

They perched together on the edge of the bed, which faced a diminutive writing desk stacked so high with papers and books that it looked like it might buckle under the weight. It was hard to imagine Cam's tall frame fitting comfortably at something so petite, clearly meant for a lady who better suited the name Camellia. Ada pictured Cam at something like a sturdy oak library table, polished to a warm amber.

"It's tiny," she said out loud, and Auggie's eyes followed hers to the desk.

"Well, it is, isn't it? I never noticed before, as many times as I've been here." It sounded as if he'd frequented Cam's bedroom, and that made Ada's hands go clammy.

"Ooh, you are nervous," he said, dropping her hand. "I understand, honey, truly."

She scanned his face for a hint that he did, indeed, understand. His eyes were a delicate green, like the leaves just starting on the willow oaks, and his nose was dusted with freckles. A thin gap separated his lips, from one front tooth that stuck out a little farther than the other. It was an endearing flaw, something folks probably didn't notice until they were up close.

"Let's take a walk," he said.

"Now?" She wondered what was going on in the other room, if folks were talking about them or if the conversation had flitted to something else. She pictured Cam casting glances down the hallway, but maybe she was so involved in talking to the woman who'd left behind her lipstick that she didn't even notice their absence.

"Why not? I didn't much like the book, did you?" Auggie said. "A little boy and two old ladies who make potions? Ho-hum. That's why I didn't finish. Let's go see something that's tons more interesting."

Ada wiped her hand on her skirt just before he grabbed it again and headed for the hallway. "We shall return!" he called to Cam, who seemed to be listening to a story Twig was telling, but whose face registered bewilderment and something else, almost like pain. Still, she lifted her punch cup toward them in a half-salute.

"Where are we going?" Ada asked when they were on the sidewalk. Voices and laughter from Cam's porch drifted like petals to the street.

"I love this street, don't you? It's so elegant . . . in a shabby kind of way."

Ada had never thought of the boulevard as anything but grand. The streetcar suburb of Dilworth was quite a few rungs above her parents' neighborhood of North Charlotte, which was the very definition of shabby—houses never stood higher than one story and yards were red clay that turned to slop in the rain. Having four or five rooms instead of the standard three was considered deluxe. Here, in contrast, roofs kissed the trees, climbing two stories or more. Instead of narrow roads where cars took turns to pass, Dilworth boasted a paved boulevard and wide sidewalks with room to breathe. The air was purer, too, at a greater distance from the cotton mills.

They had walked silently for one long block when Auggie broke into a happy trot and pointed with excitement. "There it is!" A sprawling white frame bungalow, set back from the street and guarded by a majestic oak, came into view. With its modest height and lack of trim, it was not the peer of its neighbors, but Ada recognized its charm even if she didn't understand Auggie's excitement.

"It's pretty," she said.

"That, dear librarian, is where Carson McCullers lived, oh, twenty years ago," Auggie said with a sigh. "She started writing *The Heart Is a Lonely Hunter* right there in that house."

"Gosh," Ada said. "I thought she was from Georgia. I didn't know she ever even lived in Charlotte."

"Neither did I," Auggie said. "Cam's the one told me. She's a font of obscure knowledge."

Ada pictured Cam's intent gaze when she was speaking about something with authority. "Thank you for showing me, Auggie. I just love that novel."

"We should read it for the next installment of the book club, don't you think? Carson has such a deep appreciation for freaks." Ada smiled at the tender way he emphasized *freaks*.

"I'm not sure it's the right thing for me. The club, I mean, not the book. Though I do appreciate you going to all this trouble to be so sweet to me." He was still mesmerized by the bungalow. "I'm just not . . . I'm not sure I'm like y'all."

That broke the spell. "Why, sure you are, honey." It was so matter-of-fact, Ada felt she might believe it, too. "Why else are you spending so much time with our Cam? Why aren't you out there finding yourself a diamond ring instead? How old are you anyway?"

"Twenty-three."

Auggie clicked his tongue. "You better be careful. Old maidery is just around the bend."

"So my mama tells me," Ada said, smiling.

"She likes you so much," Auggie continued after a pause. He didn't have to say her name; a ripple of excitement traveled up Ada's arms from her fingertips just the same. "You're all she talks about these days. I haven't seen her so peppy since Viv." He dropped the name lightly, like a handkerchief slipping out of his pocket. "She made this little book club just for you. How else do you get a librarian to come over and meet your friends? She would have preferred a softball team, that's for sure."

His words made her forget the name *Viv*. Ada could hear her heart pumping. It wasn't that she hadn't considered she might be different. But twice before, she had dismissed her crushes on women as something she'd outgrow in time. One was understandable—a schoolgirl infatuation with Miss Ruthie, who treated her with respect and caring. The other was Natalie, and she was much harder to brush off.

"Do you ever wish, well, that we could be more to each other?" Ada had ventured once with Nat, when they were flopped across Ada's dorm-room bed after a perfectly lovely day of doing nothing but being together. She wasn't even sure what *more* would be, but at that moment she would have been willing to experiment.

Ada's eyes traced a crack in the ceiling as she waited for Nat's response. "Whatever do you mean?" Nat said, sitting up and smoothing her skirt. "We're close as sisters. There's nothing more to be." Uneasiness sliced through Nat's voice, and it wasn't long after that she started seeing Hank in earnest. He'd been just a casual date up till then, but by the end of the term, she was wearing his grandmother's diamond.

Now, when Ada got letters from Nat, she still felt a dull ache, like a tooth on the verge of going bad. It had been hard to hear that there was a baby on the way.

Hank and I are over the moon! Nat wrote to break the news. *My prayer is that you will know this same happiness soon, Ada dear.*

Had she found happiness, she wondered, and just didn't want to face it? The men she met were dull or patronizing, while she wished her coffee conversations with Cam would never end. It was a feeling that seemed more profound than Nat's comment about Hank when she got engaged: "He suits me, and he'll be a good provider."

"You want to head back?" Until Auggie handed her a handkerchief from his suit-coat pocket, she hadn't realized her eyes were filling up.

"Oh, Auggie, I am too mortified." She bit her lower lip and forced herself to say, in a hushed voice, "Can I ask you something?"

"Shoot."

"Are you . . . with Twig? I mean, are you two together?"

His chest puffed out a little. "A year this June."

"And is your life together . . . hard?"

Auggie took both her hands in his—such a sweet gesture that if someone had passed them on the street, they might have mistaken them for lovers.

"Honey, he's the best thing about my life."

Ada withdrew her hands after a moment and removed a pen and her prized notebook from her pocketbook. She ripped a sheet clean out and awkwardly started to write on it. Auggie interrupted her, offering his back as a makeshift desk.

When she finished writing, she creased the paper into fourths and pressed it into Auggie's palm. "I can't go back there. Not today. But please give this to Cam, and don't you dare read it."

Making the trek back across town on the bus, Ada imagined Cam's reaction. She pictured her anger when Auggie came back alone, her refusal to take the note he handed her. Finally, she'd slide it into her pocket with a scowl, maybe tell herself she'd toss it out unread. Not until everybody had left and she was alone in the apartment would she take it out and unfold it. Maybe she'd read it twice. Would she understand? Would she throw it away, or would she smile and make a call?

The phone rang at Ada's house a little before ten. "Who's calling at this hour?" she heard her mother ask. "Some folks have to work in the morning!" There was a muted exchange before Ada heard her mother's footsteps outside her bedroom door.

"Ada Jane, there's someone from school who says she needs to talk to you. Seems right urgent to me. Camellia Somebody." Ada opened the door to her mother's curious look, the one that questioned why she couldn't just be like other girls. "Isn't she the one you had supper with not too long ago?"

39

Ada waited until her mother went back to her bedroom before she picked up the receiver. "Cam? Is everything okay?"

Cam's voice was a husky whisper. "Auggie gave me your note."

The message she'd written had been simple but heartfelt: *Cam, I'm new at this. I need to know this is serious for you. I feel a lot for you, but I'm not sure what that means. Love, Ada.*

She had faltered with the closing, thinking *Yours* too suggestive, *Best* too cold. *Fondly* sounded like somebody's great-aunt Maybelle. So she scrawled *Love*, and then her hand trembled as she signed her name, making each *a* more rounded and the *d* more squiggly.

Now Cam was still talking, but she sounded far away, like she was calling from the coast. "I would never rush you. I know it is a lot to think about. But darlin', I have never felt this way about anyone. Ever."

Ada paused. The tube of coral lipstick flashed into her mind, the way it had claimed its space in the medicine cabinet. She imagined Cam leaning in to someone's lips. "Ever?" she asked with caution, aware her mother might be listening.

Ice rattled on the other end of the line. "I have been in love," Cam said slowly. "I'm not saying you're the first. I'm just saying . . . all I mean is, this is different."

"And your friend Lu?" She hesitated, twisting the phone cord.

"Oh sweet Jesus, no! Lu Pardue is a friend, nothing more. I swear to God."

"Don't swear," Ada whispered. "I believe you."

A pause stretched into ten seconds, twenty or more. Cam said something about meeting the next day after school, just to talk, and Ada shivered with the anticipation of it. She had set something in motion, and the funny thing was, the fear had left her. All she felt now was a mixture of joy and relief.

A Normal Life

1960

Ada

The ride into Davidson took them down streets of elegant old manses, but somehow Ada had expected Cam's family home to be less imposing. When Cam pulled the Plymouth to the curb in front of a stately white residence with a red-ribboned pine wreath in each window, Ada's throat went dry. The modest mill house she had lived in since birth would fit into this building three or four times, possibly with room to spare.

"I can't go in *there*," she said.

Her fear didn't seem to faze Cam, who simply lit a Lucky and said, "The house won't bite."

House was hardly the right word. Ada hadn't seen anything so grand since she was at school in Chapel Hill. But it wasn't so much the physical building that terrified her: She couldn't imagine finding things to say to the people who called such an opulent place home.

So even after Cam hopped out and hauled the suitcases onto the sidewalk, Ada was still sitting resolutely in the passenger seat with the door closed. Cam tapped on the window, and she lowered it with reluctance.

"I guarantee you my folks'll notice if you don't come in for two whole days."

"You said they had money, Cam, but *this*."

"Oh, the college built this back in the day," Cam said, as if two stories and a wraparound porch were nothing of note. "Daddy doesn't own it. He just gets to live here while he chairs the department. Lord, darlin', my old man worked his way through graduate school. Mama's the one comes from money. If you think this is too much . . . well, remind me never to take you to *her* family's place in Savannah." Cam opened the passenger door for her. "This is no big deal, I swear."

A Negro answered the front door in a tuxedo and white gloves, and Ada swallowed hard. In her change purse, she had stashed a slip of paper like an emergency insurance policy, with their friend Auggie's phone number on it. "Honey, if you feel too out of place, I'll come get you in a heartbeat," Auggie had offered. Twig had gone to family in the mountains for Christmas, leaving him on his own in his tiny apartment, and Ada knew the weight of the holiday was bearing down on him, too.

"Merry Christmas, Miss Cam," the butler said. "And this must be Miss Ada. Merry Christmas to you, too. Let me grab those bags."

"I can manage, Samuel," Cam insisted. "I'm guessing we're in my old room."

Samuel looked bewildered. "Miss Daisy said put Miss Ada in the blue room," he replied. "Mattie's got it fixed up special."

Ada read the confusion on Cam's face. She had assured Ada they'd be in the same room, that whenever she had come home from college with roommates or friends, they shared her big four-poster. ("Mama thinks nothing of two girls together," she'd said.)

"I thought we'd be doubling up, what with Lily and Parker and the little one here, too." Cam's tone sounded insistent, like she expected Samuel to change her mother's arrangement on his own.

"Miss Lily and Mr. Parker are at Miss Kathryn's," Samuel explained.

"Much to my chagrin," came a silken voice from across the foyer. "I would have loved to have both my girls under one roof again, but I didn't want us getting under each other's feet." It seemed unlikely in such a big house, but Ada doubted anyone challenged Mrs. Lively's directives.

"Merry Christmas, Mama!" Cam said, going in for a big squeeze. Ada watched as Cam's mother air-kissed her instead, protecting the thinning pageboy that was so teased and sprayed it resembled a helmet. It had likely been blonde at one time, like Cam's, but the color now had more brass to it than honey.

"Oh, we just do not see you enough!" Mrs. Lively said, holding Cam by the hands and taking full stock of her. "When was the last time?"

"Must have been Daddy's birthday," Cam said. "Mama, this is Ada Shook, my very best friend in the world. Ada's the school librarian at Central. We met on her first day, and we have been fast friends ever since."

Ada smiled tightly, wishing Cam would stop emphasizing their closeness. She wondered if Cam's mother had already intuited something about them, and that was why Ada was sleeping in the guest room.

"Aren't you darling," Mrs. Lively said. Ada couldn't tell if her eyes were just naturally twinkly or if she was tearing up a little. "And what stunning hair!" She reached out to finger one of Ada's locks, which she wore down when she wasn't at work. "What do they call it—cinnamon?"

"It's not from a bottle, Mama," Cam said.

Mrs. Lively's intimacy with her was unexpected, even though Cam had warned her that her mother "might try to swallow you whole." When Ada pressed her about what that meant, Cam merely smiled and said, "You'll see."

"Thank you for inviting me, Mrs. Lively," Ada said, to shift the focus off her appearance. She instinctively used her church voice. "This is such a beautiful home. I was almost scared to come inside!"

Cam's mother gave her a curious look. "Did Cam tell you?"

"Tell me . . . ?"

"That the place is haunted."

"Why, no, I just meant . . ."

"Because it is, you know. The people who lived here before us. He was the chair of Philosophy, and she . . . well, she slit her

43

wrists in the bathtub, poor thing. I replaced it when we moved in because it seemed like bad luck."

"Mama thinks most places are haunted because she's from Savannah," Cam said with a wink.

"No, Camellia, I have *heard* her. She calls out 'Charles, Charles!' At least, I think that's what she's saying. The husband married a bit too soon after her death, if you know what I mean, but he came to no good in the end." She paused for effect. "Incinerated in a fiery car crash."

"How terrible, Mrs. Lively!" Ada said.

"Please, dear, call me Daisy, everyone does. Now why are you still wearing your coats? And those suitcases should go upstairs. Samuel, would you mind?"

"This isn't Tara, Mother, I can carry our bags," Cam said, still clutching the handles.

"Don't be flippant with me, Camellia," Daisy said. "Samuel makes a fair wage, don't you, Samuel? Now come with me. Mattie's made canapés and a big batch of milk punch." Daisy took Ada by the arm, her grip almost urgent, and led her into what she called the "parlor," as if it were a century earlier.

Ada's eyes wandered the length of the room, from the baby grand and nine-foot Christmas tree at one end to the floral-upholstered sofa and chairs at the opposite. There was a tasteful fire in the hearth—not too low and certainly not roaring, but just enough to give the room a rosy warmth.

"Sit right here next to me," Daisy said, pulling Ada onto the sofa. "Camellia, I'm going to ask you to serve us some punch, if you don't mind, honey."

"Where is Daddy?" Cam asked, as she ladled out three cups, but Daisy ignored the question.

Ada saw Cam sneak a swallow and then refill her punch glass. The more time they spent together, the more she noticed how much Cam drank—when she was happy, when she was nervous, when she was mad; just about any time, really. It took quite a while for her to get drunk ("I've got a hollow leg," Cam liked to brag), but there were times when she clearly was. On New Year's

Eve a year earlier, she'd actually run the Plymouth up onto the lawn in the front yard of her apartment building, flattening a holly bush.

"Bring those here, and don't you get ahead of us," Daisy said.

Cam delivered the drinks, then went back for a tray of deviled eggs, candied pecans, and shrimp salad on toast points. Ada took one hesitant sip of the punch and set the crystal cup politely on the table.

"Oh!" Daisy said, after her first taste. "Mattie has outdone herself. Just the right amount of bourbon."

"Could use more, you ask me," Cam said.

"Don't you like it, Ada?" Daisy leaned into Ada, closer than was comfortable, as if she were her oldest and most cherished friend. It was an education for Ada, who now understood where Cam had learned her way of drawing people in.

"I'm not much of a drinker. I get that from my mama, I guess. She's a staunch Methodist."

"Well, no harm done," Daisy said, but Ada wasn't sure if she meant about rejecting the punch or being a Methodist.

"Where *is* Daddy?" Cam's head turned again and again toward the French doors, like it was on a swivel.

"Well, now, you have hurt my feelings. I haven't seen you since summer, and all you can talk about is where your father is."

"I'm sorry, Mama," Cam said automatically, making Ada wonder how often she apologized to her mother for such small slights.

"Anyway, your father called a while back and told Samuel he'd just be 'two shakes.'"

Cam groaned. "Well, we all know what 'two shakes' means."

"Let it go, Camellia. Your father works very hard."

"Even on Christmas Eve?" Ada ventured.

"My husband would work Christmas Day if our girls weren't here," Daisy said. She tugged down the sleeves of her angora sweater and smoothed her skirt, picking at pieces of lint that only she seemed to notice. "Last month, I called the English Department secretary and actually made an appointment to see him!"

Her laugh sounded scratchy, like a worn record. "He did not appreciate the humor in it, I can tell you that."

"I think I'll just go to the study for a minute and call him," Cam said, popping up. "He needs to get himself home."

Ada shot Cam a look that beckoned her not to leave, so Cam motioned for her to come along "to see the rest of the downstairs."

Daisy tugged at the sleeve of Ada's dress. "Why don't you stay, dear? I haven't gotten to know anything about you yet."

"We'll be right back, Mama," Cam said.

In the foyer, Cam grabbed Ada's hand and they crossed to a room clearly decorated for a man, with leather chairs and polished mahogany bookshelves built right into the walls. With the door closed behind them, Ada sank into a chair and let out a gust of a sigh. "I was terrified you would leave me alone with her," she whispered. "She's so . . ."

"Needy?"

"I would have said lonely. I wonder what she does with your daddy gone so much."

"She redecorates a lot," Cam replied, dialing. "That parlor we were in? Five times in ten years at least. And she volunteers at this and that. That kind of thing." The rings were audible through the line—five, then six, Ada counted. "What is taking so long? I'm sure he's right there, re-reading *The Great Gatsby* and swigging back some bourbon."

"He drinks at work?"

"Oh, they all do. Occupational hazard."

Her father finally answered and Cam held out the receiver so Ada could hear his booming voice. "Darlin'!" he said. Then she pressed it back to her ear and listened, a smile creasing her face.

"Maybe Ada and I should come to you. I'm sure she'd like to see your office. . . . Oh, all right, Daddy." The frown that had just started on Cam's face deepened. "We'll see you in two shakes."

Cam explained that her daddy's two shakes always ended up being more like an hour, and she couldn't bear the thought of spending all that time with her mother. She made their excuses to Daisy and said they needed to unpack. "Mama dresses for dinner," she said on the way up the staircase. "It's that Savannah thing. I'm just going to throw on a skirt instead of these old slacks, but you look absolutely wonderful. As always." Ada didn't have a well-stocked closet, but she was proud of the fact that the dresses and skirts she did own were nicely made and complimented her figure. Her black wool sheath was new this year, bought on layaway at Belk's and paid for in three installments.

"Flattery will get you everywhere," Ada said with a coy tug at her new pearls, an early present from Cam. In the time they'd been dating, Ada felt more at ease with flirting, something she had been clumsy about in the past. Cam just seemed to bring out the coquette in her. Ada's words had the desired effect: Cam cast a glance downstairs to the foyer and, when the coast looked clear, pecked her on the mouth.

"Cam!" she said, pretending outrage but feeling excited.

"Come here." Cam took her by the hand and led her into one of the bedrooms, giving the door a light kick to close it. She pushed Ada against the wall and kissed her, hard and insistent. "I have been wanting to do that ever since I picked you up and saw you in those pearls. I would love to see you wearing nothing but."

"Should we be doing this here?" Ada asked between kisses that threatened to rub her lips raw. They had so few private moments; she tended to fret about what her mother would think if she were at Cam's apartment too often or too long. But she was twenty-five and in love and craved more moments exactly like this one.

"Absolutely," Cam said, tracing Ada's neck with her lips.

"Cam, we shouldn't." But at the same time, she let her tongue find Cam's and didn't pull away when a hand made its way to her breast. Ada closed her eyes and made a little animal-like noise that Cam seemed to coax out of her, halfway between a moan and a gasp. She felt almost dizzy with the pure joy of it.

Then with horror, Ada heard the distinctive squeak of a door opening and clicking closed again, and her eyes popped with fear, her nails digging into Cam's forearm to stop her.

"Cam! Somebody just opened the door! Oh, I told you this wasn't a good idea!"

"Let's hope it was Mattie," Cam said. "She pretends she doesn't see half of what goes on around here."

Cam entered the hallway, but left the door slightly ajar. Ada heard a high, girlish voice, probably Cam's younger sister. Lily had sent Cam a recent photo in which she looked like a blonde Jackie Kennedy in her pillbox hat and two-piece suit. In her arms, she held a chunky, solid-looking baby. "His legs look like sausages," Cam had remarked, claiming she couldn't even remember the child's name.

"Lil . . ." Ada heard her say.

"Don't think I won't tell them," Lily said. "You think I'll go on keeping your little secret, but this is just too much. In their own house, Cam!"

"It's not what you think . . ." Cam began, but it was a weak rebuttal. Because it was exactly what Lily thought, what anyone would have thought if they'd stumbled onto two women in an open-mouth kiss. Lily must have found Cam's words ridiculous, because the next thing Ada heard was the click of high heels, a baby's gurgles trailing off.

Back inside the bedroom, Cam's face had lost its usual ruddiness. "You should have seen the look she gave me."

"We should leave."

"Why don't you just wait in the guest room for a little?" Cam suggested. "I'll see what I can do to fix this."

"Cam, there's nothing to fix. What's done is done. I want to leave."

"Not yet."

There was no way she was going to be able to look at Cam's parents after this, no way she could see the revulsion on Lily's face firsthand. If Cam wouldn't consent to leave, she would take Auggie up on his offer. "You can stay then, but I think I might call Auggie. He said he'd pick me up if I needed him to."

Cam's eyebrows lifted. "You didn't tell me you arranged something with Auggie."

"I'm sorry. I was nervous about meeting your folks."

Cam got a Lucky out of her coat pocket and looked like she was going to light it, but instead stuck it behind her ear. "Look, Ada Jane, I think we should live together."

Ada started at the non sequitur. "Why on earth would you say that now?"

"We act like horny teenagers the minute we're behind closed doors," Cam said. "But we're adults, for God's sake. Adults kiss and make love in their own homes, whenever they want to."

"We're not like most adults, Cam," Ada said.

"So we're stuck with . . . this? We've been sneaking around for almost two years, and this is where it's brought us."

Ada sighed and adjusted her dress, which felt like it had gotten twisted during their embrace. "Living together is a big step," she said, brushing past Cam into the hall.

Cam

Cam didn't go downstairs immediately. Instead, she stood at the top of the stairs, like a girl eavesdropping on her parents, listening for the voices below. Everything was too quiet, too calm. Beads of sweat rose at her hairline, even though the air in the hallway was nippy. She finally heard her father come home and call out, "Cam darlin', where are you?" before Samuel's soft voice steered him into the parlor.

Cam leaned on the banister and waited for an explosion. She didn't think of herself as timid. At work, she spoke up at faculty meetings, challenged the principal when she could, tried to be an advocate for the children. She'd attended more rallies and marches for the civil rights of Negroes than she could count. But at her parents' home, she was a coward, just like her father, who snuck off to his office and pulled a bottle from his bottom drawer. She'd never understood his absence, his seeming discomfort in his own home, but she'd come to think of it as the way of married men.

49

The door to the parlor opened and closed with a soft click, but she couldn't see who emerged. It might have been Samuel or Mattie, but the footsteps sounded too light for either. As the sunlight began to shift and fade, she thought maybe she should just escape back to the city with Ada, walk right out the front door. But her feet wouldn't take her anywhere, not even down the stairs. She lit the cigarette she'd stuck behind her ear, even though her mother forbade smoking in the house. As a distraction, she tried to recall the names of the books on the shelves in her daddy's office, and which order they were in. He had a compulsive habit of alphabetizing them by author. "Agee, *A Death in the Family*," she said aloud, between puffs. "Anderson, *Winesburg, Ohio*."

"Miss Cam." Mattie's voice was behind her, at the top of the service stairs. Cam turned toward her sturdy outline, but it was too dusky to make out the look on her face.

"Mattie!" She spun around, guilty about being caught with the cigarette. "Sorry about this smoke. I will get rid of it right now." But there was nowhere to stub it out, so she winced and bore the pain of extinguishing it with her fingertips.

The housekeeper's eyes were cast down. "Your daddy's wanting you downstairs. I got no idea what this is all about, but I do know dinner's going to be late for sure."

"I'm sorry, Mattie. I'm sure you worked hard on it."

She was close enough now to see lines creasing Mattie's forehead. "My Deborah's coming in from Greensboro tonight," the housekeeper said. "Samuel's supposed to pick her up in an hour at the station."

How many times, Cam wondered, had this happened to Mattie? White folks had arguments or got into sticky situations, and expected Mattie's life to go into a holding pattern.

"Maybe we could just go ahead and eat," Cam suggested. "I'll talk to mama. There's no reason to delay you and Samuel because of our foolishness."

"That would be a right uncomfortable dinner," Mattie said. "No way is your mama going to agree to that. You go on now.

50

They're in the parlor." And then she turned and hastened back down the service stairs.

Cam knocked on Ada's door before answering her parents' summons. Ada was seated in a blue chintz chair with a standing lamp shining onto the book open in her lap. "Can we leave?" she asked. Her face looked pink and strained, as if she'd been crying. "Is it over?"

"It's just starting," Cam said. "But please don't call Auggie. Give me more time."

§ § §

Samuel or Mattie had removed the milk punch and canapés from the parlor. Cam's mother wasn't drinking anything, and her father had a glass of straight bourbon that he finished and quickly refilled. Lily and the baby had disappeared, probably to her father's study. No one offered her anything, not even a seat.

"I'm afraid we won't be having dinner after all," Daisy said. She pulled a handkerchief out of the sleeve of her sweater and blew her nose daintily. "Your father would like to talk to you, Camellia." Then, to her husband: "I'll be with Lily."

When her mother withdrew, Cam sank heavily onto one of the chairs. She could see her father pouring himself a third round. When he finally turned to face her, his eyes glanced off her face and toward the fireplace. The flames were no longer perfect; the logs would need stoking or replenishing soon, or the room would take on a chill.

"I know a doctor," her father said, strained and out of nowhere. The words appeared to cost him more than he wanted to pay.

"I don't . . ."

"A very good doctor. Here in Davidson. Your mother and I will pay for it, of course. We thought you might even come home for a while. To stay. Get a leave from school."

"I don't need a doctor, Daddy."

"I beg to differ," he said, meeting her eyes. Sometimes, especially when she hadn't seen him in a while, Cam found it disconcerting how much she looked like him—the same square jaw, the sandy wave of hair, the hazel eyes with flecks of gold. When she was growing up, friends of the family remarked that it was almost as if Daisy had nothing to do with Cam's birth at all, as if she'd sprung from her father's head like Athena.

"What I meant was I don't *want* a doctor," she corrected. "I've known about myself since I was little." That wasn't something she'd verbalized before, not even to Ada or any of her gay friends, and it felt freeing to say it right out loud. Being that way was part of her fabric, a differently colored thread seen by anyone who chose to, but which most people's eyes would just skim over. "I don't see what a doctor would do about it anyway."

He sat across from her on the sofa and examined his drink, its level again low. She thought she should offer to replenish it so she could help herself to one; she needed it so badly, she could almost taste it warming her throat. But the silence in the room didn't last long.

"You'd be amazed," he said, as if he had personal experience with psychiatry. What her father said next set the room to spinning. "You know, I had ... inclinations. When I was a graduate student, before your mother and I married."

Cam wasn't sure where to look, so she focused on her hands, which she realized were gripping the arms of the chair. "I saw a doctor, and things got better," he continued. "If I hadn't done that ... well, there's no telling what would have happened. Now I'm not saying you'll change. I'm just saying you'll be able to have a normal life. A family. A home." He waved his glass in a small circle, indicating the grand parlor that he went to such great pains to avoid. "Of course, you're an adult, and I can't force you to do anything. But there could be ... consequences." The way he lowered his voice, almost as if *consequences* were as dirty a word as *queer*, made her think he was talking about money. Her parents subsidized the rent that would have been a stretch on a teacher's salary.

Her father was now a dizzy blur to her. She wanted to stand up and leave the room, she badly needed to see Ada, but she was afraid of falling over, of not even making it as far as the door.

"I have been able to show enormous self-restraint over the years, and all thanks to the doctor. I am proud to say I have been faithful to your mother."

"Faithful," Cam repeated, numbly.

"Yes, faithful. I have held up my end of our agreement." The words sounded so formal, like marriage was no more than a signed contract. Her father stared at his empty glass. "Where is your friend?" he asked suddenly.

"Upstairs in the guest room. Her name is Ada. She wants to leave. In fact, if I don't go to her within the next few minutes, she just might call a friend of ours to come pick her up."

He stood and walked to the bar cart, splashing more amber into his glass. "Another strong-willed girl. Well, you can't leave on Christmas Eve," he said. "I've . . ." He stopped, as if weighing his emotions on a scale. "I always look forward to seeing you, Cammie."

Cam felt a sharp jab in her gut. No one called her that but him, and he hadn't done so in many years. She remembered what Ada had observed the first time she visited her apartment: "You have a lot of photos of your father." Cam had denied it at first, then laughed and acknowledged that she did indeed. He had been everything to her, but now? To think that he actually understood her feelings, had felt them himself, but expected her to extinguish all passion from her life. It was like he had a grip on her innards and was twisting them this way and that.

"I'm leaving, Daddy," she said, standing up.

He nodded, making no attempt to stop her and not bothering to repeat the offer about the psychiatrist. She suspected her father would drink himself into unconsciousness that night, then stagger into his study and fall asleep in a chair. He'd done it many times when she lived at home. Tomorrow, he wouldn't remember much of what he'd said, but a vague sense of unpleasantness would linger in his mind.

Ada

Ada couldn't wait in the guest room any longer. She had tried to read, but she ended up counting the thin stripes in the wallpaper over and over. Finally, she hauled her suitcase into the hallway and listened from the landing to the peculiar stillness of the house. The French doors to the parlor were flung open, but she couldn't hear any voices, so she assumed that whatever had taken place between Cam and her parents was over. She hoped Cam hadn't been so rattled that she'd sped off without her.

With her coat on and suitcase in hand, Ada stole down the staircase. The study door was closed, shutting off the possibility of using the phone in there to call Auggie. She reasoned that in such a big house there might be another phone in the kitchen, and she turned in the direction she imagined that room would be—toward the back, tucked out of sight. But as she did, an over-sized man she recognized from Cam's photos emerged from the parlor. She had startled him, and he almost dropped a full glass of bourbon.

"Oh!" Ada said. "I was looking for the kitchen." She tried to steady her voice by enunciating each word.

"You must be Ada," he said in a melodious baritone, a speaking voice that Cam said helped make him popular with students. "That's right, isn't it? Ada?"

"Yes, sir."

"I'm T.J. Lively." He proffered his free hand, but Ada just nodded as she continued to grip her suitcase and her purse. "Well, you know that already," he said, tucking the hand back into his jacket pocket. He couldn't be too angry if he was trying to shake her hand, but Ada wanted nothing more than to disappear into the wallpaper.

"Well," he repeated, motioning roughly with his glass so some bourbon spilled onto the foyer floor. "The kitchen is that-a-way."

"Do you . . . know . . . where Cam is?"

A door clicked open behind her and Cam appeared from the study, looking as washed-out as a ghost. "I'm here," she said. "Just let me get my bag."

When Cam barreled up the stairs, T.J. bent over and mopped up the drops of liquor he'd spilled with his handkerchief. He went over the spot twice, even though he seemed to get the splatter with the first swipe. "That was an accident waiting to happen," he announced when he finished, with a feeble smile that suggested Ada was his accomplice. For several moments they both stood frozen in place, like mannequins in a store window. Then Cam was at her side, saying in a hoarse voice, "Let's go," and they left without another word.

"Aren't you going to tell me what happened?" Ada asked as Cam loaded the trunk.

"On the ride home," Cam said, her emphasis falling on the final word. It was hard not to notice, because since Ada had known her, she'd been in the habit of calling her parents' house *home*.

Cam didn't bother to warm up the car, but instead pulled away while Ada's breaths were still moist clouds. When she finally spoke, the darkness of her tone scared Ada, like the times she went one drink too far, beyond her happy stage and into a black funk.

"So I'll tell you this, and then I don't really want to talk about it anymore," Cam said. "Daddy and Mama want me to be 'fixed' by a doctor. I said no. He said he's been through it and it worked wonders."

Ada blinked hard a few times. The news was too dramatic to let ride between them like a silent third party. "What on earth do you mean, he's been through it?"

"Seems he's queer as a two-dollar bill."

Ada tried to absorb that, how Cam's father could be married and a homosexual at the same time. They had two children. "I just can't believe that," she said.

"And why would I lie?" Cam's tone turned sour, and Ada watched her hands tighten on the steering wheel. She didn't want to fight on Christmas Eve, but Cam seemed more than ready for it.

So Ada stared out the passenger window, her mind filled with the Davidson house, the perfect log fire, the pristine tree, the French doors, and then the drops of bourbon glistening on the oak floor, Cam's father wiping them up. She would ask Cam at another, safer time what exactly had happened in the parlor, but now she knew it was best to keep still. When they had both been quiet for a few long minutes and Cam's hands seemed to relax, Ada reached over and flicked on the radio, where a local station was playing Christmas carols that filled up the void.

As the lights of Charlotte flickered and drew closer, she wondered what they would do the next day for Christmas. The last thing she wanted was to be deposited at her parents' house on Christmas Eve. "I told you it was wrong to leave family on Christmas," her mama would say. Ada would sulk alone in her room, then go to church with her parents the next day, pick at Christmas supper. It was hard to imagine anything lonelier.

And what about all the Christmases to come? A sense of panic welled up in Ada's throat. Family was what you did on holidays—gathered with your folks or the folks of someone close to you. Unless like Auggie—and now, it seemed, Cam—you were unwelcome even among the people who raised you from a child.

They were just a few blocks from her parents' house when she glanced toward Cam and said, as gently as she could, "Honey, I don't want to see my folks just now. Let's go to Auggie's."

Cam opened her mouth like she might protest, come up with some reason for being alone. But she closed it again, and without even a slight acknowledgment of Ada's suggestion, she made a right turn where she shouldn't and they headed in a new direction.

The Plan

1962

Auggie shot himself on a balmy day in May. Ada had stayed late at school to assist two girls researching their American literature projects. They sat with *Encyclopedia Britannica* volumes splayed open on a scarred oak library table. Their teacher had assigned Herman Melville and Edgar Allan Poe, claiming only male authors were worth studying.

"Now I would have picked different writers," Ada said. "You ever read *The Member of the Wedding?*"

"No, Miss Shook."

"*To Kill a Mockingbird?* That just got itself a Pulitzer Prize, a very fancy award."

Two sets of blank eyes stared back at her, so she returned to her desk. She was drawing up a list of books to include in a new bulletin board display when she noticed Cam in the library doorway, waving through the window for her to step into the hall.

"Shouldn't you be at practice? Or did you miss me that much?" Ada said, looking up and down the hallway to make sure they were alone. If the library had been empty, she might have ventured a kiss on the lips, too, just to feel the forbidden spark of it electrify her body. They were at long last moving in together at the end of the term. Cam's apartment had two bedrooms, conveniently located at opposite ends of a hall so it would look like they were just roommates.

Cam, who was usually full of saucy comebacks when Ada flirted with her, seemed more than a tad distracted.

"Darlin'," she said, her eyes round as hula hoops, "I've got to get back to the girls, so I'm just going to come straight out with it. Something bad's happened to Auggie."

The words that tumbled out didn't make sense to Ada. She stared at Cam's mouth like someone trying to lip-read.

"... shot himself," Cam seemed to be saying. "This afternoon. Right in Twig's living room. The police are there. Twig's gonna need a place to stay for a few days, so I offered him my couch. I hope that's okay."

"I don't understand. Where's Auggie?"

"Oh lord, darlin'. He shot himself in the head with that revolver Twig kept—the one belonged to his daddy? Blew his damn fool brains out."

§ § §

In April, the *Observer* had run the story, below the fold on page one. Accompanying it was a grainy photo of young men being escorted into the police station, their hands in cuffs, heads turned away from the camera to conceal their faces. "10 Arrested in Homosexual Round-Up." Auggie's name and address topped the alphabetical list—Augustus F. Barkley, 30, 820 Catawba Ave., Charlotte, N.C.

Before school in the library, Cam had read the story aloud in a hushed voice, and Ada's stomach flip-flopped. "Seems like some kind of crackdown going on. Remember they raided Neptune a couple of months back?"

"But why do they print the names?" Ada asked. "Isn't being arrested bad enough?"

"Not by half," Cam said. "It's the humiliation, darlin'."

Twig had posted bail, even though they were just friends now and not lovers, so Auggie was home by lunch. The following Monday, the manager at his bank called Auggie in and handed him his slip. No two weeks' notice, no pay for unused vacation days, not even a "thank you" for eight years of service—just a curt goodbye and dismissal. "You see the position we're in," the manager said.

"Missionary, obviously."

Ada gasped when Auggie related the story to her later. "You did *not* say that!" She wasn't sure if she should be proud or mortified.

He admitted he hadn't, that he only thought of it later when he was already through the revolving door. Ironically, Auggie said he hadn't planned on cruising that night. The city was having a rainy spell, and "Who wants to get down on your knees in the mud? I mean, what a *mess*." At the last minute, though, the sky cleared, and the stars flickered like lightning bugs. "I wish to God it had stormed," Auggie said with a sigh.

The snappy retorts Auggie was famous for—Cam dubbed him Oscar, for his one-liners—became fewer and further between as the weeks went on. His eyes took on a glassiness that reminded Ada of her Uncle Rad, who had returned from the war in Europe with what everybody called "battle fatigue."

On an evening when Ada knew Auggie was at home, he didn't even pick up his phone. She imagined him passed out on his sofa, butts and empties strewn around him. "He'll burn his place down if he's not careful," she said to Cam as she replaced the receiver in its cradle. "Should I go over there?"

"He's a grown man, darlin'," was all Cam said. It was hard to see him that way. Although he was a few years older than Ada, she felt like his big sister, offering comfort and company when he needed it. Even his carrot-top hair stuck up in a cowlick, the way her brother Foster's did when he was a kid. Auggie had no family to speak of; his daddy had tossed him out right after his high school graduation. But it wasn't something he dwelled on. Ada only found out when she innocently asked if his parents were proud of his promotion to chief teller at the bank. "Couldn't say," he said, sniffing. "They disowned me years ago. You're my only real family, you and Cam . . . and Twig, even though he broke my heart."

She had heard about other fellows like Auggie who had given up, "accidentally" plowing their cars into trees or fashioning nooses out of belts, at the very time they should have been launching their lives. But though Auggie had seemed down, he hadn't registered as despairing. He still got up every day, took a shower, talked to his defense lawyer, checked the Help Wanteds in the *Observer*. Who bothers to look for a new job if he's going to kill himself?

In fact, Twig said later, Auggie had been so relaxed when he arrived at his house that day, Twig thought he might have actually turned the corner on dejection. "I opened the door and he just said 'hey' in his usual way. He acted so calm, said he'd come up with a plan—no, he called it *The* Plan. I asked if he wanted to go to Shoney's and tell me all about it, 'cause my shift didn't start till four. I went to change into my scrubs, so I could go to work right from supper . . . I wasn't gone more'n ten minutes, I swear to y'all . . . and that's when I heard it. I seen a lot in my days, but nothing like that. His . . . well, it was all over the walls." Twig's hands covered his face, like he was trying to erase the picture from his mind. "My neighbor heard the shot, so she called the cops. She said I screamed, but I don't remember."

That night, Ada slept over at Cam's, making up an excuse for her mother about a friend "in crisis." From the sofa where he slept, Twig let out a piercing wail in the pitch dark that jolted her and Cam awake.

"Shouldn't we go out there?"

"He's going to have nightmares for a while," Cam said.

Cam's matter-of-fact way about the ordeals of life struck Ada as cavalier. What happened to you just happened, Cam seemed to think, and you were better off moving on as fast as you could. Ada, on the other hand, was accustomed to accompanying her mother when she brought casseroles to grieving neighbors, praying along with widows whose hearts were shattering right in front of her.

"Well, I can't sleep now," Ada said. She slipped Cam's bathrobe over her chemise, and swept her hair back with a rubber band. In the dark, it was hard to distinguish Twig's willowy frame from the shadows. When she sat down beside him, Ada could see beads of sweat glistening on his face in the moonlight.

"I can't get it out of my head," Twig said, his mountain twang more pronounced when his guard was down. Then out of nowhere, "I wish I could take it all back."

"What do you mean?" She thought she should stroke his arm or back, but she had never been one to touch or hug. Even with Cam, she sometimes went stiff if the embrace went on too long. She wished Cam would come and hug him for her. But one thing she was good at was listening.

"I cheated on him, Ada."

"Oh, he told me that, honey. That's not why he did it."

"I know," Twig said, the tears rolling freely down his cheeks. His voice got more high-pitched as he continued. "But I still wish I could take it back! The other fellas—they were *nothing*! If we were still together, he wouldn't have gone to that park—he wouldn't have, I know it! I know it for a fact!"

Her hand went out tentatively and skimmed the layer of black hair on his forearm. She had no experience with men, and the silky feel surprised her. She imagined hair that thick would be coarse and nasty, and cause her to recoil. Instead, she settled into a rhythm of petting him like her neighbor's retriever.

"You can't do this to yourself," Ada said. "People don't just . . . do something like that unless they're troubled in their minds. I kept asking Auggie to come to church with me, but he wouldn't."

"What good would church have done?" Cam said from the bedroom doorway. "It's not like God is stepping in to help the *homosexuals*." She pronounced it in the way she did when she was being sarcastic, stringing it out into its full five syllables.

Cam's blasphemy never failed to prickle Ada, and faith was a roadblock they still hadn't made it past in their four years together. Like her folks, Ada was a lifelong Methodist, while Cam was a proud agnostic.

"Hush," Ada hissed. "We all know how you feel about God. Now please go get Twig a glass of water."

Cam lit a cigarette first, and the tip glowed orange in the darkness. She inhaled deeply, as if making some sort of point, before heading to the kitchen. Ada turned away, her attention focused again on Twig, whose chest was heaving in and out with great effort. She leaned in and whispered, "Would you like to pray with me?"

Twig's head bobbed like a puppet's, and she took his hands in hers. "Dear Lord," she said, bowing her head, "we pray for our sweet brother Augustus. Please forgive him his sins and welcome him into your kingdom, so he may find rest in your loving arms. We pray for this in the name of Jesus Christ your son, who gave his life that we might live."

A glass made a distinct "clunk" on the coffee table in front of them, and Ada pressed her eyelids down more firmly, blocking out Cam's disapproval. "We thank you, Lord, for each other, and for the precious gift of life you have given us. Please help us keep Auggie in our hearts and prayers. For this God is our God forever and ever; he will be our guide even to the end." She heard Cam take another long drag. "Amen."

"Amen," Twig repeated after her. He opened his eyes a second after she did and downed the glass of water in front of him in a single gulp.

"Being who you are is never a sin," Cam noted, crushing her cigarette into an ashtray.

"You know I don't think that," Ada said.

§ § §

Auggie's death notice read, "Suddenly, on May 14." There was no visitation listed, no funeral, no way to show respect for their friend. Twig contacted the funeral parlor to find out if there had been an omission in the paper, but was told "the deceased's family" had decided on a brief, private service.

"Probably just tossed him in the ground," Twig said through bursts of tears.

Twig decided to stage his own late-afternoon service, when the cemetery would be quiet and there would be few to notice. Auggie deserved a real party, he said, so he placed phone calls to "a few dozen of the finest homosexuals." He even bought balloons, but only Ada and Cam showed up.

"The fellas are scared," Cam said. "You can't blame them."

Twig wore his charcoal go-to-church suit, with matching orchid shirt and socks and a white carnation in his lapel. It was hard to find Auggie at first, but then the Barkley plot appeared, replete with marble tombstones elaborately carved with Biblical verses. One grave had freshly turned dirt, with a wooden cross at its head that obscured its owner's identity: A.F.B., 1932–1962. Twig wailed at the sight of it.

"At least they did the right thing and included him with the family," Ada said, patting his back. "You sure you want these balloons, Twig? It might not be ... respectful of the others."

"The others can go eff themselves," Twig said, wiping his nose on his sleeve as he draped balloons from several trees. "Pardon my *French*."

In the end, Twig's service was a serene affair and not much of a party. Ada read Psalm 130 and found her voice surprisingly strong: "Out of the depths I cry to you, O Lord, Lord, hear my voice! O let your ears be attentive to the voice of my pleading. If you, O Lord, should mark our guilt, Lord, who would survive? But with you is found forgiveness: For this we revere you."

Twig invited them each to say a few words about Auggie, and Cam was the first to think of something to say. After remembering happier times—meeting him when she opened a bank account, sharing a cottage at Folly Beach—she ended with, "I'm sorry you're gone, my friend, I'm sorry you were in so much pain. But this ... this really ticks me off!" Ada grabbed her arm, urging her to stop, but Twig chimed in, "How could you do this to me?" Their reactions made Ada's left eye twitch, and she declined to speak.

Finally, on a portable record player, Twig played "Stand By Me" and sang along with Ben E. King in a slightly off-key baritone.

Ada had one white rose for Auggie's coffin, and she placed it on the mounded dirt before leaving. At the shop, the florist had given her a sly grin and said, "One perfect rose for your sweetheart?" Ada didn't know what to say, so she just agreed: "Yes, ma'am," and hurried out, forgetting to take her change.

"Rest, Auggie," she whispered now. "I hope for your sake it's in peace." In her mind, Ada added, "I love you," something she was too shy to say to him when he was alive.

Twig suggested supper at Shoney's, but when their order arrived, he picked at his fries and ate the pickle off his burger, and Cam had a few bites of her club sandwich. All Ada could tolerate were some sips of a ginger ale. Even that roiled in her stomach until she thought she might toss it back up.

Later, Twig went home. "You been good to me," he said, hugging Cam, "letting me stay so long. I just couldn't face that room, but . . . well, it's time."

As they approached the intersection for Ada's house, Cam asked if she wanted to spend the night. Stopped at the traffic signal, Ada watched it turn from green to red through the windshield. She wanted to ask Cam what she thought happened after death, but was afraid of her answer.

"I best go home," was all she said, the desire to be alone sitting like a river rock on her chest. They didn't speak again, except to say goodnight, and Cam brushed her cheek with dry lips.

"Saved you some chicken and greens," her mother called out to her, as if it were just another day. Ada went to her room and closed the door with a gentle click. She fell asleep on top of her grandmother's quilt, even though it was just past six.

§ § §

At breakfast, there was a note on the kitchen table: "Camellia Lively phoned," in her mother's crisp, schoolgirl penmanship. Ada could read the parental disapproval in just those three words.

"I don't know why you spend so much time with her," was her mother's continuing complaint. "Unless she's working on finding you a husband. You know, your window of opportunity won't be open much longer, Ada Jane!" Ada was almost twenty-seven and knew her mother actually feared the window was closed for good.

That morning at work, Ada found herself avoiding the teachers' lounge and the cafeteria—any place she might run into Cam. They usually tried to find ways to bump into each other during the school day. But since Auggie's death, they'd been snapping at each other more than talking, and the only thing that registered now when she looked at Cam was disappointment.

When Cam stopped by the library after classes to ask if she'd be coming over that evening, Ada begged off, saying she'd gotten her period and felt poorly. "I'm not good company."

"Since when do we only see each other when we feel good?" Cam asked. "I thought we were way past that."

"I guess I just don't want to." When hurt filled Cam's eyes, she added, "Be with anyone, I mean."

"Even me."

Especially you—but Ada couldn't say it. The truth was, she wondered now if she could be with someone who had so little faith, who didn't believe in the grace of God. Ada went to church every Sunday, even when she'd been out the night before, and attended Wednesday evening services when she could fit them in. For a while, she'd been in the church choir, until the rehearsal schedule became too onerous.

"You mean you *still* read the Bible?" Cam had asked when they first became friends. "Even though no one makes you?"

"His word helps me," Ada said, feeling self-conscious about her beliefs for the first time.

Cam softened her stance. "Well, whatever gets you through."

Their different takes on faith cropped up from time to time, especially when Ada left Cam's bed early on a Sunday to go to services. "It's too hard to explain to someone who's basically a heathen," Ada had barked one morning early in their relationship, when she'd had her fill of Cam's attempts to detain her.

Cam lashed out. "I have my own kind of faith! Sorry it's not the simple-minded 'Whatever you say, Jesus' kind you Shooks subscribe to!"

Ada stormed out, slamming as many doors as she could. That first breakup lasted a week, until Cam apologized for calling Ada's faith simple-minded. "But I need you to accept that I'm a believer in my own way. *I* have faith, too, just in different things. I have faith in you, for example. I have faith that people are good underneath. I have faith that Negroes and gay folks and all the other outsiders might be let in someday."

It sounded pretty, but Ada didn't cotton to alternative kinds of faith. And now, when all she had to get her through Auggie's death was prayer, she was having a hard time even looking Cam in the eye.

"Maybe we should take a little break," Ada suggested, her voice wavering as she tacked up pieces of a display on summer reading. "Maybe I shouldn't move in just yet."

"Why would you do that?" It wasn't a demand so much as an entreaty.

"So I can get things straight in my mind," Ada said. The thumbtacks didn't go in as smoothly as she would have liked, and a few dropped from her shaking hand. Cam retrieved them and handed them back gently, and Ada noticed that she was close to tears. She had only seen Cam cry a couple of times— once, in sorrow, when her granny died, and once, in jubilation, when President Kennedy was inaugurated.

"What's to get straight? We have a plan!" Cam said. "We've talked about this for almost two whole years, Ada Jane, we've fantasized about living together. I'm sick about Auggie, too, but I just don't see why our plans have to change!" The use of her name instead of the usual *darlin'* was jolting, unfamiliar; and Cam's voice, so forceful and shrill, was the kind that invited attention. Ada glanced toward the library door window and thought she saw a figure darting away. Being found out was a fear that had taken up residence in the back of her mind.

"Because I have my doubts about the whole thing," she replied. Then she turned back to her display, knowing she hadn't been clear about what "the whole thing" was—the apartment? Their relationship? Being a gay girl? So the argument dangled like a worm on a hook until Cam finally turned and left.

§ § §

66

At supper, her mother filled up the silence, rambling on about the high price of beef, the words Clay Junior's baby girl had learned that day, the new folks at church. Ada let her drone on, not even attempting to insert an observation or chuckle, the way she might when she wasn't feeling down. She ate just enough so her mother would think she was watching her waistline, not being torn up inside.

Her father made swift work of his meal and left the table for a smoke on the back porch, while Ada's mother glowered after him. "That man's not said ten words at supper in a year. But you? The cat must have got your tongue."

"Just a little tired, Mama. I'm sick."

Sick was the code word her mother had devised for having her period, something she could say at home in front of her father or two brothers to avoid embarrassment.

Her mother tilted her head. "You been like this for almost a week. Being sick should be over by now."

"It's nothing to trouble yourself over."

"You're no trouble to me, Ada Jane. You can always talk to your mama." But her lips were pressed together, as if she feared what the invitation for Ada to unload her worries might bring. Ada hesitated, considering how to break the situation into bits her mother could swallow.

"Mama, you know I was planning to be roommates with Cam Lively come the end of the school year."

A pinched look crossed her mother's face. "And I'll repeat that I think that's plain foolish. An unmarried girl, no matter how old, should be home with her folks." Ada's mother had married at seventeen, gliding easily from her parents' home to her husband's.

"I know what you think. But if I changed my mind . . . if I decided, say, I couldn't afford it, or just didn't want to right now . . ."

"This will always be your home," her mother said a bit too eagerly, already humming a tune as she packed leftovers into the Frigidaire. She would likely come up with a new man for Ada to meet at church, a widower with thinning hair and a houseful of another woman's kids.

§ § §

Ada came home from school late on a Thursday, and Twig's Chevy pickup was parked in front of her house. "Thought you were still on the night shift," she said through the open passenger window. Twig worked as a hospital orderly, but did not have his scrubs on, and an old duffle bag was secured in the truck's open bed.

"I'm leaving, Ada," he said. "Going to Atlanta for a change of scene. I got a cousin there who said I could crash on her couch."

"You're leaving *now*?"

"I thought you might have a drink with me first. One for the road, as they say." He leaned over and popped the door for her.

She stepped up into the cab, casting a glance toward her parents' bungalow. She thought she saw the curtain in the front room sway.

"My mama's hopes will be up. She'll think I finally nabbed myself a beau."

Twig laughed so hard his head snapped back. "You'd have to be right desperate to take up with someone like me." He liked to denigrate his looks, because he was tall and angular, with a chin and nose that looked like an amateur had sculpted them. But he'd had no trouble finding lovers, and he had started mentioning a man named Jimmy.

He drove her to The Hornet's Nest, a bar in the basement of an old hotel in town. It wasn't a homosexual club so much as a place where gay people gathered while the management turned a blind eye. Both women and men frequented it, and Cam had accompanied Auggie and Twig there many times, against Ada's advice. The place seemed seedy, dangerous, with an entrance down a dark flight of stairs. "And what if you run into someone from school?" Ada had asked.

"I reckon they'll be as scared to see me as I am to see them," Cam replied.

Twig ordered a shot of whiskey for himself and a Coke for Ada, and he sat across the table from her, eyes focused on the door.

"You expecting trouble?" she asked.

"Always. Mind if I smoke?" He tapped his pack of Luckies on the table, and as if on cue, Cam appeared from behind them and pulled out the chair next to Ada's.

"If I had known . . ." Ada said, the color rising from her neck until her ears felt like they were on fire.

". . . you wouldn't have come," Twig finished.

"Are you even *leaving* town? Or was that a bald-faced lie?"

"I am for a fact, for a long weekend. Now if you ladies'll excuse me, I should be hitting the road." He downed his shot and was gone.

"Don't be sore at Twig," Cam said. "I asked him to trick you into coming, and he owed me one."

"If I wanted to see you, I would have called," Ada said.

"Darlin', please, I'm dying here. I don't know what it is we're doing, what I did to make you not want to see me. All I know is I'm lost. It's like somebody took my damn head off and screwed it back on the opposite way."

Ada smiled in spite of herself, feeling something loosen inside her as Cam laid a hand on top of hers.

"Can you at least tell me what I did to hurt you? Hell, Ada Jane, I'd even go to church with you and ask forgiveness from God Almighty if it'd make things right again."

"I would almost believe you," Ada said, "if you hadn't said 'hell' in the same sentence as 'God Almighty.'"

At the sting of her words, Cam removed her hand and laid it flat on the table with its mate. She shrugged. "You know that's just me, darlin'."

Ada examined the veins that roped across Cam's hands, then let her eyes travel up to the muscles in her arms, so pronounced from playing sports for twenty years, ever since she was little— everything from softball to basketball to volleyball to golf. "The only balls I ever knew a damn thing about," Cam liked to quip.

She finally met Cam's eyes. She'd looked into those eyes first as a friend, later in times of passion. She'd studied the flecks of gold in the hazel until the pattern was as familiar as her own name. The fact was, although they would likely always fuss and fight, Cam's were still the only eyes she wanted to look into every day.

She reached over and put her hand across Cam's. "I *have* missed you," she admitted. Then, so she wouldn't appear to be surrendering too much too easily, she added, "Sunday service is at eleven."

Trouble

1970

It turned out there was no bomb, but the scare was bad enough. Ada had been leading a class of seventh-graders in a lesson about the school library's resources when the fire alarm sounded, a string of unrelenting staccato beeps.

The librarian knew very well it wasn't a drill. The paper had reported that in the first week of classes, nine public high schools across Charlotte closed for bomb threats, although no actual explosives turned up. White and black parents alike were vexed by the judicial busing order. "My child is simply not riding a bus for an hour," one angry white mother told the reporter.

Ada's twenty students remained oblivious, ecstatic that class was cut short. They laughed and tripped over each other on their way out to the parking lot. "Quickly now, children," she instructed as she tried to shape them back into an orderly line. "Let's *go!*" Her voice was more urgent than she intended, but they were taking their sweet time, and what if this threat was real?

"Well, isn't this a fine how-de-do," Cam whispered as they stood side by side in the parking lot with their students. "I told you the crazies wouldn't just target high schools."

The parking lot was the farthest point from the school building. Three or four car lengths away from them, standing with his eighth-grade class, was Robert Browne, the new history teacher and the junior high's first full-time black faculty member.

"I wonder how Mr. Browne feels," she whispered back.

"Same as us, I expect," Cam replied. "Damned embarrassed to live in this city. I can't help thinking back to those bombings five years ago. You remember? When they blew up the civil rights workers' homes?"

Mr. Browne was the replacement for a white history teacher who had retired abruptly rather than work in a school that admitted more than just a few token blacks. Several others had followed that teacher's lead. The number of white students had diminished, too, with dozens of parents withdrawing their children and enrolling them in segregated private academies.

The new teacher was younger than both Ada and Cam, no more than thirty, and wore his hair in a close-cropped Afro. Unlike Mrs. Prescott, the part-time music teacher who could almost pass for white, his skin was dark as coffee. He seemed to have one good gray suit that he freshened every day with a crisp striped shirt and pocket handkerchief. No matter how sweltering the day, his suit jacket stayed on. Ada recognized him as a fellow introvert, somebody who kept his distance out of habit, but maybe he was more outgoing among his own folks.

"Mr. Browne has a sterling academic background, top of his class at Johnson C. Smith," Principal Riordan announced during in-service day. The principal had never praised the credentials of any other new teacher, as far as Ada could recall, and Mr. Browne looked embarrassed. "I hope you all will join me in welcoming him to the Central family." The staff offered a round of applause, but later Ada overheard some ugly talk. ("He's so ... *black*," one teacher commented. "Like a field hand," another agreed.)

"He's a good-looking man," Ada noted while the faculty and students waited in the parking lot for further instructions.

"Can't say I noticed," Cam replied. Then, with a grin: "You switching teams on me, darlin'?"

When the police arrived with their dogs, even the youngest of the students sensed the danger. The parking lot became a sea of fidgeting bodies, with some students crying like elementary school children.

"Everything's fine," Ada said to reassure her class. But then Principal Riordan's voice came over a bullhorn: "Due to unforeseen circumstances," he said, "we are ending classes early today."

All month, Central endured bomb scares that amounted to nothing, but still, the threat of trouble fell like gauze over the start of the school year. Teachers were less companionable, rushing to classes and then home directly after, instead of tarrying to socialize in the lounge. Students seemed fussier, especially in the cafeteria, where petty skirmishes erupted. Principal Riordan now had a full cohort overseeing lunch, two faculty members and an assistant principal.

Ada was paired with Jeanette Hutchins, the new P.E. teacher she and Cam had both wondered about—"You think she's one of *us?*" they'd asked each other—but who sported a gaudy diamond on her left hand. Miss Hutchins liked to insert some tidbit about "my fiancé, Tom," into conversation whenever she could. "The butch lady doth protest too much," Cam liked to say. Still, she was a compatriot in politics, if nothing else. "I just don't see what the fuss is about," Miss Hutchins said of the changed makeup of the student body. "They're children, for goodness sake."

Cam's partner on lunch duty was Mr. Browne, and she expressed an eagerness to get to know him better, even under tense circumstances. If anyone could get a shy person talking, she could, her ease with conversation having first drawn Ada to her. In just a few lunch periods, Cam learned that Mr. Browne had been arrested in a Charlotte lunch counter sit-in in 1960 and had taken part in the Freedom Rides a year later as a card-carrying member of SNCC.

"He helped make history!" was the way Cam put it, delight spreading across her face. She had a progressive streak a few miles long, especially when it came to civil rights. They weren't so far apart in their beliefs, but Cam took her actions further than Ada was willing. "Isn't that a Negro event?" Ada had asked when Cam expressed interest in going to the March on Washington in '63.

"It's for everyone, Ada Jane," Cam snapped. In the end, Cam

had traveled without her, on a bus chartered by a local Presbyterian church. "It was a once in a lifetime event," she said on her return, "and you missed it."

"Next time," Ada replied.

Now, it seemed, there was always something more to report on Cam's growing friendship with Mr. Browne, who had glided into being "Robert." "I invited Robert to lunch at Anderson's," Cam said after supper one evening when they were reading across from each other in the living room. Ada was absorbed in *Slaughterhouse-Five*, while Cam was finishing up *The Death of the President*. The announcement came out of the blue. "This Saturday."

Ada felt a pinch of jealousy. She liked Anderson's, a popular restaurant not far from school frequented by Central teachers and staff. Why hadn't Cam invited her? Saturdays were a golden time when they slept in late and then went to movies, or held at-homes with their gay friends.

"You could invite him here instead," Ada suggested. "I have a ham."

Cam's book closed with a soft slap. Her hands busied themselves smoothing the cellophane that covered the library book.

"That's not a good idea, darlin'."

"After all these years I think we know how to be discreet."

"I didn't mean *that*." Cam put the book on the end table and hunched forward in her chair. "I meant, you don't see any blacks in this neighborhood. Except for Pinky." The gray-haired handyman came Monday afternoons to mop the floors of their apartment building and drag the trashcans to the curb. Even though Ada asked him to call her by her Christian name, Pinky steadfastly added the "Miss" in front of it.

"With all the trouble that's going on in the city, it'd be even less welcoming around these parts for Robert."

"Yes, of course," Ada agreed, embarrassed that she had only considered her own feelings, not Mr. Browne's.

She waited to be asked to Anderson's, too, but instead Cam cracked her book open again. It was only when she had put it aside to get ready for bed that Cam added, "You could come along. To lunch, I mean. Unless . . ." Her voice trailed off, and Ada knew the invitation was insincere.

"No, you go," Ada said, struggling to soften the sharp edge of her voice.

Later, Cam brought home a piece of pecan pie for Ada and didn't have anything special to note about the lunch date. "It was fine," she said. "I told Robert we're roommates, and he said to tell you hey." But she was all animated energy until supper, suggesting to Ada that *fine* had been an understatement.

§ § §

On a quiet morning when there'd been no bomb threats or fights in the cafeteria for at least a week, Robert Browne came to the library and cleared his throat until Ada took notice.

"Mr. Browne," she said. "How can I help you?"

"Robert," he corrected her. "I want to order some books. For the library." He placed a loose-leaf sheet in front of her. "I checked the card catalog and didn't find any of them." She scanned his handwritten list, which included titles by W.E.B. DuBois, Frederick Douglass, Booker T. Washington, and James Baldwin. The library had no titles by black authors save a dog-eared copy of *A Raisin in the Sun,* which Cam taught in eighth-grade English.

"Absolutely," she said. "High time we integrate this library."

But at the bottom of Mr. Browne's list was a more worrisome choice—*Invisible Man* by Ralph Ellison. Ada hadn't read the novel, but had skimmed reviews and knew it could be controversial for its sexual references and profanity, coupled with the fact that Ellison had Communist ties.

"This Ellison book—maybe you should run that by Principal Riordan," Ada said. She tucked an errant lock that had escaped her bun behind her ear as she leaned down to make check marks on the sheet.

"Why's that?"

"Well, exposing students to certain things could be touchy, is all."

"So Central has a censorship policy?"

"I should say not!" Ada said, indignant and flustered at the same time and unable to meet his eyes.

Cam must have informed him that Ada ruled the stacks. In her thirteen years as librarian, she had never asked any teacher to get the principal's permission to order a book or periodical. But then, they mostly ordered books Ada could personally vouch for.

Mr. Browne was also requesting a subscription to *Ebony*. An inspirational magazine seemed harmless on the face of it, but the memory of Miss Ruthie still flickered in her mind. When Ada was in high school, Miss Ruthie had been fired from the public library for bringing supposedly subversive publications to her stacks—including *Ebony*.

That was 1950, though—the McCarthy era, not 1970. The world had changed in significant ways, and with it, Central Charlotte Junior High. It was true that, despite integration, black students still sat apart from white students, but it seemed to be from choice, not deference. Now they acted like they belonged and didn't seem to care if white kids saw them as interlopers. "Black Is Beautiful" stickers cropped up on notebook covers. Why shouldn't the black kids have access to books that reflected their history and culture?

Still, Ada didn't want to invite trouble in these turbulent times. All it would take was one white student checking out a book his parents didn't approve of or another one telling her folks about a photo she saw in *Ebony*.

"I'm just trying to avoid . . . embarrassment," she said.

"Mine or yours?"

The sharp question brought heat to Ada's neck, making her wish she could undo a button.

"Look," Mr. Browne said, his tone edging toward conciliation, "I'm just trying to follow protocol, not step on any toes. I showed the list to Cam—Miss Lively—just the other day, and she told me to bring it straight to you. You two are roommates, she said."

Ada nodded, thinking, *Cam should have warned me.*

"She said there would be no problem. So forgive me if I don't understand. Do you tell all the teachers the same thing?"

How could she explain the situation after the fact to Mr. Browne, without sounding like a bigot? Which she most certainly was not. Hadn't her mother set her on the right path when she came home from first grade singing the song she'd learned at recess, about catching niggers by the toe? Much later, intense discussions with Cam had expanded her thinking about racial injustice. Some of their most earnest conversations when they were becoming friends and later lovers had been about segregation.

"I *have* questioned other books," Ada said. It wasn't a bald lie: She remembered asking Cam why two copies of *Catcher in the Rye* were necessary. "But tell you what. Let me go ahead and put your order through. My intention was not to offend you, Mr. Browne. It's just . . . I know this school. I've been here since the very first black child enrolled. I know these students and their parents."

His face registered curiosity, like he was trying to decode her. "But we have new students and parents to think about, don't we?" he asked. She wondered how many black parents would be happy with the content of *Invisible Man*, but that was a question she couldn't ask.

Mr. Browne held her eye and then lightly tapped her desk with his index finger before turning to leave. "I've taken enough of your time."

They'd gotten off on the wrong foot, and if Cam found out, there would be hell to pay. She needed this young man to know she wasn't like other whites, the ones who touted their Confederate ancestors or acted like Jim Crow was still in force. She could have used the example of Miss Ruthie to explain away her cautious behavior, but it seemed like too elaborate a story, offered too late. Or she could have told him about the early days of integration at Central, but she had done so little—just interrupted one bullying incident.

So instead, she said, "I . . . I've read Mr. Baldwin," just before he reached the library door. Cam had brought the novel *Giovanni's*

Room home from her trip to Washington, D.C. for the March. "It's about two men who have an *affair*," Cam had explained excitedly. "One white and one black." The volume had made the rounds in their gay circle before ending up, tattered and well-read, on a high shelf in the bedroom closet.

"He's a fine writer," Ada said.

"One of the best," Mr. Browne said, with a thin smile that suggested he might not hold a grudge. "You have a nice day now, Miss Shook."

"Ada," she said.

§ § §

When Mr. Browne's order arrived, Ada catalogued and shelved the books herself instead of assigning the task to her volunteer library assistant. It wasn't that she didn't trust Mrs. Randolph— she was, after all, one of the community members who had escorted black students from their buses to their classrooms on the first day of school. But Ada figured the less attention drawn to Robert's order, the better.

Ada slipped a note into his mailbox, letting him know that the titles had arrived and were available for borrowing. Within a few days, eighth- and ninth-graders were asking where they could find *Up from Slavery* and *My Bondage and My Freedom*.

"I don't think we have that, dear," she heard Mrs. Randolph say when a girl asked for the most recent issue of *Ebony*.

"Mr. Browne said you did."

"I'll handle this, Mrs. Randolph." Ada stepped in and directed the girl to the periodicals. Later, she explained to the volunteer that the library was now carrying the magazine, and that it had probably first come in on Mrs. Randolph's day off. "It's right there, above *Life*."

"Well, that is wonderful for the children," Mrs. Randolph said. "I will make a note to recommend it."

Given the popularity of the books and magazine, Ada spent some time researching novels and poetry by black women writers, too—Maya Angelou, Dorothy West, Gwendolyn Brooks, Paule Marshall. She compiled a list and placed it in Robert's mailbox with a handwritten note: "I thought the girls might like these, but I haven't read them myself. Could I ask your opinion?"

The note came back to her the same day with a brief response. "I am not familiar with these writers."

It seemed a bit terse and dismissive to Ada, but she found it hard to gauge someone's tone through a one-sentence reply. Maybe he was in a hurry when he wrote it. Or in the worst-case scenario, maybe he didn't think women were as important as men.

"Curious thing happened today," Ada told Cam at supper. "I wanted to order six books by black women writers, and Mr. Browne—Robert—said he had never heard of them. Not a one."

Cam kept her eyes on her plate, her fork poised over her creamed corn. "I'm not sure what you're trying to say," she replied in an even tone. "For sure, you are the most literate person I know, but I sincerely doubt you've read each and every one of those six books."

The truth of the statement made Ada backtrack. "I just thought it was curious," she said.

"That a black man hasn't read every single book by a black writer? I bet he doesn't know every single black person in this town either. No more'n you or I know every gay person."

Ada traced a faded stain on the tablecloth with a fingernail. "I take your point. But just once, I wish you'd take mine." She got up, even though she hadn't finished eating, and determined never to mention Robert Browne at home again.

§ § §

Another bomb threat, and then another, interrupted a spell of peace. Principal Riordan called a special meeting of the faculty.

"I don't know why we've been targeted," he said. "We have done nothing to draw attention to our school, so it must be random." He paused to clear his throat. "Now I don't want to worry you, but I feel you should be aware that Mr. Browne and myself have received . . . threats. Of a certain kind."

Ada had been jotting a grocery list into her notebook, but she stopped and sat up straight as a flagpole. Across the crowded faculty lounge, she caught Cam's eye and could tell she was equally surprised.

"You mean death threats?" a teacher asked.

Mr. Riordan sucked in a deep breath. "I'm afraid I do, Jim," he said. His own household had endured several late-night calls, and Mr. Browne had received a letter at school. "The police are studying it for fingerprints. All this is to say that we cannot take these bomb threats lightly. I know they haven't amounted to anything anywhere across the city, but we must continue to be vigilant just the same."

The principal referred to notes he'd made on an index card. "I also want to ask you not to engage with any parents who seem angry or upset, at least not on your own," he continued. "You should refer them to me, or make sure you talk to them with me or with Mr. Baxter. We're in a delicate time right now, but, God willing, this trouble will blow over soon."

Ada had never heard him invoke God before. He shifted from one leg to the other as he spoke, beads of sweat forming on his upper lip. The pressure on him must be great, with just a year under his belt as principal. Like her, he had been in college when the *Brown* decision came down in '54 and a newly minted teacher when integration began three years later.

She thought about the library's copy of *Invisible Man*, which had so far been ignored in the fiction section. Back at her desk, she considered removing it temporarily. She actually took it off the shelf and inspected its circulation card, relieved to see not one student had checked it out. She thumbed through it quickly, then stuffed it into her desk drawer for the afternoon. Maybe she would take it home and read it herself, decide if it was as problematic as her wandering imagination feared. But at the end of the school day, she told herself she was not a censor and returned it to its place.

For Ada, Principal Riordan had been a refreshing addition to the Central administration. He told teachers to call him "Jack," was hands-off when it came to faculty, and brought new ideas from his most recent post. A few veteran teachers, however, viewed him with suspicion. "He's from *New York*!" was the charge leveled by some. "You know that old joke," Cam said. "A Yankee's someone who lives north of the Mason–Dixon line. A damn Yankee is a Yankee who doesn't leave."

So Ada wasn't expecting trouble when the principal poked his head into the library during seventh period, noted the room full of students, and asked if she had "a few minutes" to spare after school. "Stop by my office, would you? Even if I look busy, please just barge right in." There was no hint of menace in his voice, no tightened facial muscles. His tone and manner were almost breezy.

"I'll be a few minutes late today," she told Cam, who waited so they could drive home together. "Jack Riordan wants some sort of favor, I think."

"Maybe it's the chess club," Cam said. "They never replaced Burnside."

"If that's it, I'll be forced to volunteer for some other activity, like Future Homemakers of America."

"You *are* a fine cook."

"Close the door, if you don't mind," Mr. Riordan said when she appeared soon after the final bell. It was her first clue that something wasn't right; the second was that he didn't look her in the eye, but instead kept writing something on a notepad. She took a chair with a cushion that was starting to fray along the edges, and saw a copy of *The Fire Next Time* on his desk. It had the clear wrapper she put on all the library's new hardcover books, to protect their jackets.

"You know this book," he said.

"James Baldwin, yes. That looks like our copy."

"You ordered it, then."

"I did." This would have been the time to add, "Mr. Browne requested it," but she held back the information.

"Have you read it, Ada?"

"I have not," she admitted. "I have read other work by Mr. Baldwin, though, and he is a very fine writer. Clear and concise. Thoughtful."

The principal examined the book as if she had just handed it to him. "A parent brought it to me. She wanted to know what this particular book was doing in a junior high school library." Ada wanted to ask how the mother got it, but kept her silence. "I took the book home last night and read quite a lot of it, and frankly, Ada, I wonder what it's doing here, too. Not only is Baldwin overly critical of religion and of Caucasians, but I've heard he's a homosexual." The word sounded uglier than it did when she or Cam used it.

"It was ordered, along with a number of other books on black issues." She kept her words passive, as if the book had found its way onto the shelves on its own power. "No more than twenty in all. It was an attempt to integrate our library, now that our student body is pretty well mixed. The books were for different reading levels, and they all fit within the budget, which . . ." The principal held up a hand to interrupt her.

"This is a formal complaint." He handed her a typed letter. "We now have a mother with several vocal, like-minded friends wanting to inventory our entire library. They're taking the issue to the PTA. These parents want to know what the school has made available to their children."

Ada scanned the letter. *The Fire Next Time,* she believed, was a collection of essays on race. It was not a book she would have ever bothered to worry about. She had never heard it mentioned among Baldwin's homosexual-themed books. The moment when she had temporarily hidden *Invisible Man* in her desk drawer flashed into memory, along with Robert Browne's face when he said, "So Central has a censorship policy?"

"No one said these children have to read Baldwin," she said, placing the complaint back on his desk. "You know, Jack, once something like this starts . . ." She meant allowing parents to dictate which books a school could purchase. Ada had heard horror stories about school districts removing such revered novels as *The Adventures of Huckleberry Finn* and *To Kill a Mockingbird* from the shelves after one or two parents had hissy fits.

"I don't need to remind you that the PTA raises money for new books," he said. "You have to take this seriously, Ada. It is not an idle threat."

§ § §

After school, Cam and Ada sat across from Robert in one of the bright orange booths at Anderson's. Cam and Robert ordered coffee and pecan pie as if it were any day, but Ada flicked the waitress away like an annoying mosquito. She had hinted at the problem in a note to Robert, but now she laid out the scene with the principal.

"I am to appear with Jack at the PTA meeting next Monday evening," she explained. "I think there should be some sort of plan."

"Well, the plan is simple," Robert said. "I'll come and tell them I ordered all the books, including Baldwin's. I won't come out and call them bigots, but I will challenge the notion that a clearly written book by one of our leading black intellectuals isn't appropriate for students."

"Unfortunately, there's more to it than just racial bigotry."

Ada and Cam exchanged a quick look. They had never confided their twelve-year relationship to anyone except other gay people. Lying awake in the dark the night before, they had discussed the possibility of clueing Robert in, so that he could understand the depth of the problem. Ada had read a recent poll in *Time* magazine that found most Americans thought homosexuals should be forbidden from teaching or having any access to children.

"It's hard to go into detail here," Ada said, wondering why she had ever thought they could talk in a crowded diner.

Cam jumped in. "Let's just say that part of the objection with

Mr. Baldwin has nothing to do with him being black. It's something more personal. If you take my meaning."

Robert sipped at his coffee in silence.

"And this makes Ada and me . . . vulnerable."

Robert's fork skimmed the outline of his pie without cutting into it as he glanced at each of them with a puzzled look. *Please say you understand and let that be it,* Ada thought.

But instead, he shook his head. "That is not my fight." In another breath he added, "I don't think parents should be choosing what books schools buy. I will help on that end and, of course, on all racial matters, but I can't . . . I just can't defend . . . *that.*"

Ada cast a sideways look at Cam, whose face sank with hurt and disappointment. Just a few months earlier, Cam had read excitedly in *The New York Times* about a parade through the streets of New York City for gay rights. "I wish Auggie had stuck around to see this day!" she said, when she told Ada about it. "Our civil rights are coming, darlin', and it's going to be a glorious day!"

Now Robert's words separated the two sides of the table like a wall. The sounds of clanking plates and other diners' laughter filled in the silence. Robert swallowed a forkful of pie, then another, without chewing, until his slice disappeared.

"I should get going," he said, sliding a crisp dollar bill across the table toward Cam. "My girlfriend is expecting me, and she'll be fit to be tied if I'm late."

"I do appreciate whatever help you can give us," Ada added, as he stood up. He said something in parting she couldn't quite make out.

"Never mentioned a girlfriend to me before," Cam noted when he was out of earshot.

§ § §

Cam and Ada recruited about a dozen sympathetic faculty members to attend the PTA meeting, teachers who did not want parents to start scanning their assigned reading material, too. Even Miss Hutchins, who had no assigned texts for P.E., showed up. Mrs. Randolph, the library assistant, offered to come and to circulate a petition among the parents; her own son and daughter had attended Central.

"I feel horrible," she told Ada. "I checked that book out to a boy, a white boy. He and his buddy were snickering over something in the corner. I should have known they were up to no good. I am so sorry! I wish I had told you."

I wish you had, too, Ada thought. But what she said was, "I should have kept you better informed."

At the meeting, Mrs. Knight, the woman whose son had borrowed the book, brought a formal measure before the PTA, requesting dedicated time for a committee of parents to inventory the library's card catalog. The concern, she noted, was that certain books might be inappropriate for junior high students. She had become aware of at least one book written by "a militant activist who is a homosexual and atheist."

"I shudder to think what else might have slipped into the stacks," Mrs. Knight said. "Completely unintentionally, I'm sure." She cast a glance at Ada. "We don't want to disrupt Miss Shook during school hours, but we would like time after school to formally assess the library's holdings. I request a vote on this measure, which I typed up and we are now passing out to all attendees."

In the flurry of whispers as people read the mimeographed sheet, Ada noticed Robert Browne enter the assembly hall and take a seat near the back. Someone passed him a copy of the proposal.

"We will take discussion of the measure," Mrs. Gawley, the chairwoman, said.

Cam's hand shot up.

"Please don't antagonize them," Ada whispered.

"Well, I've got to say *something.*"

When Mrs. Gawley recognized her, Cam said, "Good evening, y'all. I am Camellia Lively, a Central English teacher since 1955. My word, that does make me sound old!" People laughed, and Ada sighed with relief: Cam had turned on her signature charm, and opted for "My word" instead of her more typical "Sweet Jesus."

"I am so pleased to meet you, Mrs. Knight," Cam continued, her tone shifting. "It is gratifying to know we have parents who are willing to take on the monumental task of inventorying thousands of books that have been in the library for years—maybe decades. I'm not sure you are aware that Miss Shook, our librarian, got her B.L.S.—*summa cum laude*, I might add—from Carolina. On full academic scholarship." She paused for effect. "It *is* the best library program in the state. Is that where you studied library science, Mrs. Knight?"

"Please, Miss Lively," Mrs. Gawley said. "Let's keep this respectful. You've made your point."

"No, Mrs. Gawley, I haven't. This measure is simply preposterous, that's my point. Parents can certainly choose what their own children read, but librarians and teachers are the only ones qualified to decide what belongs in our schools. The fact that one or two or three or even four parents don't like something in the stacks doesn't mean it should be inaccessible to all." A low buzz rose from the side of the room where Mrs. Knight sat with her supporters.

"Thank you, Miss Lively. Is there more discussion?"

A parent raised her hand. "Perhaps Miss Shook could explain why she thought books by James Baldwin were appropriate for children. Because there's more than one book, according to my daughter. There is also a novel called *Go Tell It . . .*" She referred to a slip of paper. "*Go Tell It on the Mountain*. I would just like to hear the reasoning."

"Miss Shook?" the PTA chair said.

All eyes turned to Ada. Her fear of addressing groups had lessened, thanks to years of teaching students about the library, but there was a dryness in her throat when she stood up, signaling she might have trouble speaking.

"First of all," she began, so softly that it barely registered above a whisper.

"Please, Miss Shook, we need you to speak up." The chairwoman passed a microphone that had been furnished in case the crowd got too big.

"First of all," Ada repeated, her voice now amplified to a boom, "I'd like to thank everyone for turning out for this important meeting. Second, to address the issue at hand . . ." She unfolded a sheet of paper and read from it. ". . . Mr. Baldwin is a distinguished American writer who has been recognized with many awards and fellowships over the course of his career—a Guggenheim Fellowship, an award from the National Institute of Arts and Letters, the Foreign Drama Critics Award, to name a few. The book in question, *The Fire Next Time,* was a *New York Times* bestseller. *Go Tell It on the Mountain* was critically acclaimed for its portrayal of black preachers and of racial injustice."

The chairwoman interrupted. "I see you've done your homework, Miss Shook. But could you answer the question?"

"I thought I was," Ada said, allowing just a shade of pique into her response. "These books are not trashy pulp. They are works of literary merit appropriate for our students, particularly the ninth graders. These books have helped integrate our library, which sorely needed it."

Mrs. Knight's hand went up. "Tell me what you make of this, Miss Shook. This is a direct quote from *The Fire Next Time.* 'If the concept of God has any validity or any use, it can only be to make us larger, freer, and more loving. If God cannot do this, then it is time we got rid of Him.' How do you think a fourteen-year-old might respond to that?"

"I'd have to read it in context before responding," Ada said.

"And here is a line from the novel, and I do ask everyone's pardon for reading such words aloud. 'In his heart there was a sudden yearning tenderness for holy Elisha; desire, sharp and awful as a reflecting knife, to usurp Elisha's body, and lie where Elisha lay.'"

"As I said, I'd want to read that in context," Ada said, her face hot with a mix of rage and fear.

Mr. Browne stood next, and he had no need of the mike to make his voice fill the hall. "As probably the only person in the room who has read these books cover to cover, I wonder if I might add the needed context?" He efficiently and succinctly outlined the novel and the essay collection in a few sentences. "Now, it is true that Mr. Baldwin is a homosexual and has written homosexual novels that are inappropriate for our students—for *any* good Christian people, really. But the books in question are not homosexual texts. If they were, you can be sure I would not have requested them for the library."

"You requested these books?" the chairwoman asked.

"I did, and a number of others by very distinguished black authors. I did not choose the titles lightly. I was looking for books that would be accessible reading and would add to our black students' appreciation of their past. I also wanted them to have to *think*. Which is something any good teacher—" He nodded toward Ada. "—or librarian—wants his students to do."

Mr. Browne removed a book from a worn leather briefcase that looked like a hand-me-down. "It has occurred to me that perhaps the works of Mr. Baldwin have been singled out tonight because he wrote a well-received and much quoted essay in which he took our city to task for the way black children were treated during the integration struggle. No one likes to have their bad behavior on public display." He cracked open the book. "Here he quotes one of the four youngsters brave enough to enroll in white schools in 1957. I'll warn you, he uses an offensive word. 'It's hard enough,' the boy said, 'to keep quiet and keep walking when they call you nigger. But if anyone ever spits on me, I *know* I'll have to fight.'" He slapped the book shut, the only sound in the hall. "To reduce Mr. Baldwin to a homosexual atheist is just an insult. In his own words, he wants to help end our racial nightmare."

"Thank you, Mr. Browne, for the context," Mrs. Gawley said. "So we have learned that Mr. Browne requested the books in question to help his students think about racial inequality, and that he considered them carefully. We have also learned that these books have no homosexual content." The chair turned to Mrs. Knight. "I am not convinced that the library needs to be immediately inventoried because of two books that aren't as problematic as we may have thought. Mrs. Knight, do we still need to bring this measure to a vote?" Ada sensed a slight emphasis on the word *need*.

Mrs. Knight whispered something to the woman sitting next to her before addressing the chair. "I withdraw the measure for now, Mrs. Gawley, thank you."

"For now?" Cam said after the meeting adjourned. "What in the Sam Hill does that mean?"

"It means we are on notice," Jack Riordan said from behind them. The principal had been awkwardly silent throughout the meeting, although Ada had seen him taking copious notes in a small black notebook. "Ada, I would like to talk to you as soon as possible about having a plan in place to address this type of thing in the future. Tomorrow, after school?"

"Don't agree to anything you don't feel comfortable with," Cam said as they walked to their car in the dark. "You can always take it to the School Library Association."

There was just one vehicle separating Robert's car from Cam's. He was standing with the door open, as if weighing whether to stick around or make a quick escape.

"I'm going to ask Robert if he wants to come for a drink with us," Ada said as they approached the vehicles.

"I'll wait in the car." Cam's tone was crisp, as if she had already written Robert off as a friend.

Ada held out her hand to the history teacher, and he hesitated before taking it. "Thank you, Robert. I am so grateful you came. We dodged that bullet, didn't we?"

"Yes . . . for now," he said. "But I wouldn't count on this being over."

"Cam and I are going out," Ada added. "I'm too wound up to go home. I would be honored to buy you a drink."

He glanced around, as if looking for Cam.

"Cam's in the car, just itching to go," Ada laughed. "Seems to have the motor running. Please come."

"Thank you, but I don't indulge."

"Well, maybe I can buy you a cup of coffee or a slice of pie," Ada said.

"I need to get home, Ada." Something in the way he said her name, with a pinch of urgency, saddened her. She foresaw friendly nods in the hallway, clipped conversations about book orders, maybe some careful cooperation on the censorship issue. But she felt certain Robert would not become her friend or Cam's.

"It's just us, I guess," Ada said as she slid into the passenger seat.

Cam didn't question it; she simply laced an arm behind Ada's seat and backed out of the tight parking spot. "Where to?" she asked.

The Language of New York

1982

Soft, dissonant music floated from the front seat of the cab. Ada eyed the driver's ID, displayed in a clear plastic pocket on the privacy partition: AZIZI, FAROOQ. In the photo, he was at least ten years younger, and now his hair had flecks of gray. She was creeping up on fifty years old herself, but she had never met anyone with such an exotic name, although more and more students enrolled at Central Charlotte Junior High had names like Malik and Destinee.

"Lu said when cabbies know you're from out of town, they take you on a joy ride," she whispered to Cam.

"Well, since we have never been to New York, why don't we just sit back and bask in the joy?" Cam said.

There weren't any sights on the drive, just miles of expressway against a dull sky, and then lines of buildings stained gray with grime. "I think this might be Queens," Cam remarked. Ada alternated between watching the road rush by and checking the meter on the cab as it clicked higher and higher. The fare inched up toward $20, and the Empire State Building was nowhere on the horizon. The trip, if Lu could be believed, might set her back a month's salary.

The cabbie turned out to be a commendable driver—no weaving in and out or near-miss accidents or crude gestures at other cabs. He even removed their suitcases from the trunk at the Hotel Pennsylvania, something Lu claimed drivers never deigned to do. "They just might drive away with your luggage still in the cab!" she had warned.

"This has been one fine introduction to the city of New York," Cam complimented him.

"Yes, thank you so much, Mr. Azizi," Ada said, hoping she had pronounced it correctly, to rhyme with "dizzy." He looked startled at first, then the corners of his eyes crinkled into a smile.

"You are from . . . Texas?" he asked.

"Charlotte, North Carolina," Ada corrected. "It is our very first time in New York City."

"In fact, it's our first trip north of the Mason–Dixon line," Cam added. "Yankeeland!"

"Ah, a very fine team," Mr. Azizi said, accepting his tip with a gracious nod. Ada caught a glimpse of Alexander Hamilton as the bill disappeared into his pocket.

"Ten dollars, Cam, really? He was a good driver, but I didn't know I was living with Rockefeller's daughter."

"It was worth it," Cam said. "Admit it, darlin'. Lu put the fear of God in you about the Big Apple, and your worries were for nothing."

"Well, let's just get through the weekend," she replied.

§ § §

Ada's experience with travel was limited to the back-and-forth from Charlotte to Chapel Hill when she was in college, jaunts to Raleigh for library conventions, visits to her brother in Charleston, the disastrous, aborted Christmas visit to Cam's hometown of Davidson, and vacations at Folly Beach. Those were plenty for her, all within a neat, three-hour radius of home. The prospect of flying to New York City for a long weekend had roused more fear than excitement in her.

On the plane, her fingers left white grooves in Cam's hand. The landing at LaGuardia made her gasp—the plane seemed poised to take a belly dive into some body of water, but a ribbon of tarmac appeared beneath the wheels just in time. Cam held her breath, too, and Ada heard her release it as they scraped earth.

Cam had tried to lure her to New York many times before, always in June, after school let out for the summer; she'd wanted to attend the city's Gay Pride event ever since she'd first read about it. She remained partial to large, "historic" events and still talked about having heard Dr. King speak the iconic words "I have a dream" (though he was just a speck from where she stood, she admitted).

"I'm fifty years old," Cam said, "and I have never been to a real-life gay event."

"We've been to parties. We've had our at-homes."

"I mean an *event* event," Cam said. "Something we could look back on and tell folks, 'We were *there.*'"

"I don't know who would care," Ada pointed out. "Except maybe Twig." She had no taste for the throngs that apparently attended the annual gay parade in New York; thousands of people on a street in a strange city was a petrifying prospect. "Maybe you could go with Twig or somebody else," she had said, thinking that their gay friend might thrill to being among so many men— all shirtless, if you believed the pictures Cam had shown her.

"I want to go with *you*. For our anniversary." It had been twenty-five years since they'd met in the hallway at Central. "Besides, you always pick the vacation—Charleston and Folly Beach. How about we do my choice this once?"

Without waiting for her permission, Cam made an appointment with Lu's travel agent and came home waving two envelopes in front of Ada. "You only have one silver anniversary," she said, "and we are going to celebrate in style." Then Cam buried the itineraries in one of her dresser drawers, probably sensing that the next words out of Ada's mouth would be, "How much is this going to cost?"

Their Manhattan hotel was nothing for picture postcards, but at least it was clean and right in the middle of the city, and when Ada inspected the towels, they weren't skimpy. At the front desk when they were checking in, the clerk didn't flinch at two middle-aged women sharing a room. "One bed or two?" the young man asked without even looking at them, to which Cam replied,

"Two, thanks. And two keys." Ada had insisted on the beds, for appearance's sake, even though the city would be "crawling with gays," according to Cam. Ada was grateful the clerk didn't ask if they were sisters, a clumsy question usually phrased in a way that was hard to refute ("Y'all are sisters, right?") and despite the fact that she was short with reddish-brown hair and a heart-shaped face, while Cam was a head taller and blonde with a square jaw. Both had an answer always at the ready: "No, we're just real good friends."

Even from seven flights up, midtown Manhattan looked like it could use a vigorous scrubbing. "Lu told me when she was here, she saw a rat right on the sidewalk," Ada noted as she scanned the scene below, New Yorkers pushing and shoving their way to somewhere else. Lu had told her plenty of things, all of which dampened her interest in the trip like a soggy washcloth. "Have your keys out at night and hold them like this." Lu had demonstrated, arranging her house and car keys between her fingers so they looked like spiky brass knuckles. "Don't be afraid to go straight for the eyes if somebody tries to mug you."

But when they took to the streets in their tennis shoes, Ada felt her enthusiasm for New York rising. There were so many landmarks she'd only seen at the movies. Macy's rose up in front of them like a tall ship. And even though Cam preferred anything to department store shopping, she agreed to a spin through the first floor—all the while dodging perfume girls who tried to catch them in a fragrant mist.

"You come out on a completely different block!" Ada marveled when they emerged through the revolving door into a bustling square.

It turned out, Cam had something better than Macy's up her sleeve, but wouldn't say what it was. They hiked several long blocks and then a few shorter ones, arriving at a majestic building flanked by stone lions. "Oh!" Ada said, awed by the words *The New York Public Library* etched into the facade.

The Rose Reading Room was the very definition of "library." The ceiling mural and chandeliers, the polished tables equipped with lamps, the dumbwaiter that transported book requests from deep in the bowels of the city . . . this was truly a story to tell at the next meeting of librarians she attended.

Cam suggested she peruse the card catalog and order something from the stacks, "just because we can"; she could thumb through it at one of the reading tables. "Something gay would fit the weekend," Cam proposed, but Ada thought it was rude to take up the librarians' time for a book she couldn't possibly read before closing.

"Do you think we could come back tomorrow?" Ada asked, but Cam pointed out that she had planned a full day of sightseeing for Saturday; that the next day, Sunday, was the parade; and that they were flying back that same night.

Ada was glad she'd brought tennis shoes, because they walked more than she had since she was young and living at home and eager to get out of her parents' house. After the library, they strolled Fifth Avenue all the way down to Greenwich Village, a labyrinth that wasn't as easy to navigate as midtown but radiated charm from every doorway. They made a stop at Oscar Wilde Memorial Bookshop—"Twig won't believe this!" Ada said, snapping a picture with her Kodak—then found their way to Djuna Books, a lesbian-owned shop where they spent a good hour perusing books even Ada had never heard of. Cam bought a baseball cap emblazoned with the word *DYKE* and put it on immediately. "When in Rome," she said. Ada picked out a button that read: *We Are Everywhere*, but she was afraid it would leave holes in her blouse, so she attached it to her canvas purse instead.

Out on the sidewalk, a middle-aged black woman, walking side by side with a younger one, was in mid-argument, talking so earnestly and gesticulating with her arms that she didn't notice them exiting the bookstore. Cam held up two hands to ward off a collision. "Whoa!" she called out.

"Oh, my, excuse me!" the woman said, a trace of a drawl slipping through.

Ada nodded, already getting accustomed to jostling on the

95

streets of New York, but Cam lingered, staring wide-eyed at the woman. "Viv?"

The older woman looked startled. "Lord, is that you, Cam?"

"In the flesh!" Cam took off her new cap and ran a hand through her hair. She and Viv both broke into astonished smiles. "Give me a hug, honey!"

Viv complied, and they held onto each other for several long moments in which Ada looked back and forth between them, as out of place as a vegetarian at a barbecue. She glanced over at the younger woman, who was already looking off down the street as if bored.

"What in the world are you doing here?" Cam asked.

"I've lived here going on fifteen years now," Viv answered. "Well, just across the river in Hoboken. You live here, too?"

"Just visiting. Our first time." Cam seemed to remember all of a sudden that Ada was accompanying her. "This is my . . . this is Ada," she said, waving the air next to Ada. "This is my old friend Viv."

Ada knew very well who Viv was, having long ago pried out of Cam the names of each and every lover she'd ever had. Viv had preceded her by less than a year. "She crushed Cam like a cheap glass," Auggie had confided to Ada.

"This is my daughter, Clarice," Viv said, pulling the younger woman into their orbit. While Viv's skin was the color of warm oak, Clarice's was a couple of shades darker, and she wore her hair in an elaborate composition of braids that Ada found fascinating. She wanted to ask her how she managed it, but the question seemed too nosy.

Besides, it was Viv who really held her focus. Viv was tall and muscled—a former athlete, like Cam. They'd been a couple for about nine months. "Just long enough to birth a big heartache," Auggie once said.

But she was a more stylish dresser than Cam, outfitted in contrasting shades of turquoise and rust that Ada would have never thought to put together. Her blouse and pants clung in the right places and made Ada feel self-conscious in her baggy jeans.

"So you married . . . what was his name? The businessman?"

Ada could hear the pique in Cam's voice, even though the hurtful incident was twenty-five years in the past.

"Lawyer," Viv corrected, her smile turning coy. "Roy Matthews. It didn't work out. But at least I got this pretty girl. Clarice is a sophomore at NYU. Her other mama, Gina, and I live in Hoboken."

"You already told her where you live," Clarice said.

"Well, this is just the smallest world, isn't it?" Cam was grinning like a schoolboy talking to a crush, which made Ada feel hot right through to her scalp.

"Mama, we're going to be late."

Viv snuck a look at her watch. "Well, that's the truth. We really do have to go. How long are you in town?"

"Just till Sunday," Cam said.

"Cam's got us booked solid," Ada added, so Cam wouldn't get any ideas about trying to meet up again.

"Well, I hope you have a wonderful visit."

The two exes hugged again, like a swift tug between war buddies. "Any tips on things we should do?" Cam asked as they pulled apart. "Favorite spots for gals like us?"

"You might like Ariel's," she said. "That's a women's bar on Nineteenth Street. Gina and I don't go in much for things like that, but when we do, that's where we go. The Duchess is a dive, but you might like to experience it."

With an awkward half-wave, Viv turned and strode off, Clarice tagging along behind. Cam stood planted on Tenth Street, examining her feet like they'd grown roots. "Wasn't that just the oddest thing?" she said finally.

"I don't know how odd it was," Ada snapped, "but you sure acted funny."

Cam looked up, searching her face for something. "I don't know what you mean."

Ada's irritation came spilling out. "Oh, please! You were like some love-struck teenage boy. Goofy grin and all. 'So you married what's his name?' You *knew* she did. I remember when Shirley

97

Ann told you. You sulked for days. Drank a bottle of bourbon all on your own. Seemed like you hadn't gotten over her, and you and I were together barely a year." That hurt still rankled, too: Ada had spent Cam's bender wondering if she'd made a bad mistake pairing up with her.

"I don't remember that at all." Cam frowned. "You know you're prone to exaggeration, Ada Jane." Chucking the fault onto Ada was Cam's trump card when she was cornered in a lie, but now she seemed to realize she'd taken it a step too far. "I am sorry, darlin', I don't know what came over me," she said. "I felt foolish again, like the hurt was brand new. I mean, she dropped me for a man, but it turns out she's gay after all. Ironic, huh? How would you feel if you found that out about Natalie?"

Ada had never been lovers with Natalie, her college friend, but the emotional bond was so fierce, it was like they'd had an emotional affair. The two hadn't seen each other since Nat's wedding—her husband was a career Army man, and he and Natalie had traversed the globe. Ada got a Christmas letter from Nat every year or two noting the arrival of a new baby or a change in APO address. Most recently, they'd moved just a few hours away in Fort Jackson, and the fantasy had crossed Ada's mind that maybe she and Nat could have a reunion. But then she rejected even broaching the idea—she couldn't tell Nat about Cam, and the last thing she wanted to see on her friend's face was pity that Ada had never married.

"I'd like to think I've moved on after thirty years," Ada said.

"You're a better man than I am, Gunga Din."

§ § §

As Viv had warned, the Duchess was an "experience"—a poorly lit hole with pounding music and thick clouds of smoke. "Our clothes will reek," Ada said.

From a rickety table in the corner, they watched women half their age dancing and flirting, dressed in everything from tight T-shirts to oversized flannel that resembled Ada's daddy's pajamas. The booming beat of a younger generation turned any conversation into a shouting match. The lyrics—the ones Ada could understand—were baffling. "'Come on, baby, make it hurt so good'? What kind of song is that?" She still preferred the music of her youth—Johnny Mathis, Patsy Cline. Cam just smiled, possibly not even hearing what Ada said.

Ada would have gladly left after one drink, but Cam seemed giddy as a teenager whose parents were out of town. She kept ordering, occasionally testy when she couldn't get a refill fast enough. There were so many shots and beers that Ada stopped counting. And she was used to keeping count: she had to. Cam downed as much as any man, and Ada worried about getting home safely. When Cam drank and drove, they'd had some harrowing trips, like a run-in with a holly bush one New Year's Eve, or a circuitous trip back from a party out in Matthews, taking two hours instead of the usual thirty minutes.

"I could live here!" Cam bellowed. "This place speaks my language."

"It's a right dump, you ask me." Ada replied. Earlier, in the ladies' room, a thin layer of water covered the concrete floor, like somebody had recently hosed it down.

"No, I mean New York. Maybe we should move here. You know, lots of gals from Charlotte have migrated north, like those two who put out the lesbian magazine. And Viv."

Cam hadn't mentioned Viv in almost an hour, but she was obviously still on her mind, and Ada's stomach did a little flip.

"I'm telling you, I could become a Yankee," Cam went on. "I love Yankees!" A wiry brunette wearing a baseball cap with the entwined letters *NY* glanced their way and tipped her Budweiser in their direction. "We could be *open* here, Ada Jane. New York City may be the best place to be gay." She paused. "Well, there's San Francisco, but that seems like going to another country."

New York felt like another country to Ada, but she didn't say so. "I think it's time to go have some supper before you get too rowdy, and then we should get our gay old selves to bed. We got a big day tomorrow . . . according to your own itinerary."

99

Cam agreed to leave, but only if they could make one more stop after eating—the other women's bar Viv had suggested.

"You've already had plenty."

"I am sober as a judge," Cam said, touching her index finger to her nose with care. "Humor me, darlin'."

They ate at a diner across the square from the bar, and ordered sandwiches from a waitress whose uniform was Carolina blue. Ada opened her mouth to protest when Cam asked for a beer instead of coffee, but got cut off.

"Oh, come on. It's Friday night!"

Ada could have sat in the booth for the rest of the evening, resting her feet while picking at a piece of apple pie and watching the passers-by. Every configuration of couple seemed to walk through Greenwich Village that night. She wondered if she could get used to such openness after so many years keeping her relationship under wraps. But then she reminded herself that they would never make such a drastic move because who in New York was going to hire a middle-aged teacher and a school librarian?

Cam was itching to head to the next bar, so they began the trek back uptown. The Reuben sandwich seemed to sober her up a little; her step was sure and quick, and Ada had trouble keeping up with her long strides. "Take my hand,'" Cam said, and after glancing around, Ada obliged. It made her feel almost light-headed, to walk with Cam the way married couples did and not think twice about it.

"I sure do love you, Ada Jane. You know that, right?"

She did, on a deep level, but then there had been the light in Cam's smile when she recognized Viv. Cam hadn't looked at Ada in that rapt way in many years.

"Oh, hush," Ada said. "You don't have to say it right out in public."

"There's nobody to hear it but us," Cam said. "Can't you just say it back? This is New York City!" Her voice rose on the city's name, and Ada slapped her arm and mouthed, "I love you."

And at that point everything seemed fine, even having one more drink at one more bar. But above 14th Street, the city turned into a grid again, the crowds thinned out, and the streets felt more deserted. Down every dusky side street, businesses and wholesale warehouses were shuttered for the night. If Cam noticed, she didn't say; she kept up a steady stream of chatter about the Duchess, the bookstore, and all the sights she hoped to see the next day. She didn't once mention Viv. "If we get adventurous," she said, "maybe we'll take the subway out to Brooklyn. There's a lesbian restaurant there!"

At 19th Street, Cam became disoriented and wasn't sure which way to go. Ada remembered drunken car rides at home, how Cam had insisted she knew where they were while making every wrong turn imaginable until Ada's anger exploded like a Coke somebody had shook up and opened.

"I thought you knew where we were going!"

"I thought so, too," Cam said, her voice thick with the uncertainty of one too many drinks.

"I hate it when you're like this," Ada said, dropping her hand. "If you could hold your liquor, that'd be one thing, but you go all foggy-headed on me."

"I hold my liquor fine," Cam snapped. "And *you* could be responsible for the directions once in a while."

Cam opted for a left turn, but said, "The street numbers are going up," after they passed a few buildings. "They're supposed to go down. Let's turn around."

"Oh, for heaven's sake."

As they approached the corner again, Ada saw an indistinct pair of men on the avenue, laughing and mumbling in between swigs from bottles in paper bags. Had they been behind them the whole time? "Take your hat off," she urged, but Cam left it on.

Close up, the two figures turned into gangly teenagers with pimply faces, just tall enough to have a few inches on Cam. Sixteen, maybe seventeen—an age that made Ada uncomfortable, and they were drunk to boot. The boy wearing a Motley Crue T-shirt made wet kissing noises in their direction, which his buddy mimicked.

101

"You wish!" Cam smirked, as if inviting confrontation.

"For God's sake, Cam, just shut up!" Ada chastened as she grabbed Cam's hand again and broke into a trot across the avenue that left them both breathless. Taking God's name in vain and then telling Cam to shut up were sins, she knew, but she wasn't going to think about that now. She had bigger worries. She'd made the mistake of checking back over her shoulder—just the quickest glance. The ringleader caught her look and must have decided the fun wasn't over. The two boys sprinted after them, cutting them off before they could get any closer to where a sandwich board and pulsing music indicated the women's bar.

"Where you think you're going? To the dyke bar?" the leader said, almost spitting out the words. He zeroed in on Cam, leaning forward and yanking off her cap with his free hand. He put it on his own head and made kissing noises toward his cohort. "Look at me, I'm a dyke." The other boy snickered and took a pull from his bottle.

"Okay, I don't need this," Cam said. "Recess is over. Keep the hat." Her fingernails pressed into the soft flesh above Ada's elbow as she tried to edge them past the leader. But the boy grabbed Cam by her other arm and wrenched it back hard. Ada heard what sounded like a crack and saw Cam wince in pain.

"I dunno. Maybe what you need is some cock. I never done an old lady," the boy said, still twisting. "You ever done an old lady, Pete?"

"Ah, come on, man," the other one said, like raping a woman his mother's age was the biggest bore he could imagine. He looked back toward the avenue and chugged his beer.

Ada had no time to fumble for her keys. She reached down and pulled the *We Are Everywhere* button off her handbag, bending the pin out. With one jump forward, she slashed at the leader, surprising everyone, even herself, as she drew an ugly scratch down his forearm that made him drop both Cam's arm and his beer bottle with a yelp of pain.

"You bitch!" Then, with all the force she could muster, Ada jerked Cam by her good arm and shot off in the direction of the music. "Help!" she screamed, hoping her voice would travel down the block to the bar. "Help us, somebody! Help!"

Her cry brought a stocky woman in a white T-shirt and black leather vest flying out of the bar. "Go fuck yourself, punks!" she yelled toward the boys. "Get the fuck off this street! I'm calling the cops!" The ringleader spat on the sidewalk, and hurled a volley of epithets before disappearing around the corner.

"You okay?" the woman asked. She was tough as a work boot, probably the club's bouncer.

"He wrenched my arm good," Cam said, rubbing it. "If it weren't for this gal . . ." Her face lit up with a beam of satisfaction and pride. "She went and sliced him with her gay pride button!"

Leaning in to examine Cam's arm, Ada could smell a rank mix of beer and corned beef on her breath, and her stomach wobbled.

"You were something, darlin'!"

"Don't you *dare*," Ada whispered, her heart scuttling like it was trapped in her chest. Cam flinched at the rebuke.

The woman from the bar had spiky black hair and silver earrings up and down her lobes, and her vest was studded with gay-themed pins, including one that said *Non-Breeder*.

"A pin, huh? Lemme see." The woman reached out and took the makeshift weapon from Ada. "You got some skin on it. Here, take this." She slipped a button off her vest and handed it to Ada. It was a double-edged purple hatchet on a white background.

"Come on inside. I'll call the cops. You should get that arm checked," the woman continued. "You can have a drink to dull the pain while you wait. On the house."

"No thank you to the drink, but we'll take you up on the police," Ada said. "I'd feel better if she saw a doctor."

"No need," Cam said. "Pain's easing up. Let's just go back to the hotel."

"Where you staying?"

"Hotel Pennsylvania."

"You could walk from here easy, but you don't wanna run into those punks again. I'd hail a cab at the corner," the young woman advised. "Seventh runs uptown, you'll be home in no time."

Home, Ada thought. *I wish.* These things just didn't happen in Charlotte.

She thanked the woman profusely, fishing in her bag. "I heard New Yorkers wouldn't give you the time of day, let alone save your life," Ada said, extending a ten-dollar bill with an unsteady hand. "I thought we might be killed right there on the sidewalk, and all we had for protection was some little pin. I have new respect for the Big Apple."

The woman's face scrunched up in confusion, and a dismissive *pfft* escaped her lips. "I don't take tips for basic human decency, Scarlett O'Hara," she said. "And only tourists call it 'the Big Apple.'" The woman turned on her heels and left them on the sidewalk.

"Well, I take it back. I guess New Yorkers are just as rude as Lu warned," Ada said, smarting from the Scarlett O'Hara comment. She continued to eye Cam's arm. "I don't like not getting that looked at."

"I said I'm fine," Cam said, her words turning crisp. "Don't play mama."

Ada bristled. They hadn't been talking about her drinking, but the words tumbled out of her mouth just the same. "Well, you act like you still need one. I am sick to death of trying to rein you in when you drink."

"I can control my drinking fine. I had just one too many tonight."

"This isn't the first time, Cam. It's just the worst."

"I admit that was mighty scary back there, but . . ."

"I want you to stop drinking," Ada said, surprising herself as much as Cam. The words echoed in her ears like she was in a cave. She'd made plenty of demands on Cam over the years, like getting her to church on Christmas and Easter, but never this. She had gone along with the drinking, accepting it as part of Cam's makeup or heritage, something she couldn't help because she'd learned it from an unhappy father who died with a pickled liver. But then, maybe Cam *could* help it. Ada's daddy drank, too, but she rarely touched the stuff. "I would like you to stop," she said, softening her choice of words so the notion would go down easier for Cam, like a swig of bourbon.

They stood facing off for several long seconds. Cam scratched nervously at her cheek. Ada broke her gaze and examined the pin the bouncer had given her before dropping it into her bag.

"I won't go to AA, if that's what you mean," Cam said finally, and Ada's heart picked up a beat of hope.

"Whatever you need to do." She motioned toward the avenue. "Let's go now."

Ada started walking first, and Cam followed a few steps behind, only catching up at the corner. The *DYKE* cap was tossed on the sidewalk there, like it was waiting for them, and Cam reached to retrieve it.

"Looks like you can still wear it for the parade," Ada said, taking it from her and brushing it off. Then she went to the curb and extended her arm, like a signal flag, the way she had seen New Yorkers doing. A cab flew out of a pack of headlights and swerved to meet them.

Raised That Way

1990

When the call came, Ada was sipping coffee and staring at a morning TV host whose perkiness would be cloying at any time but was downright unbearable just after dawn. In her bones it felt like a Shady Ada kind of day—Cam's name for the mood shifts Ada still suffered, even after going through the change.

Her brain was too foggy to make sense of what the journalist was saying, but it sounded like Nelson Mandela had spoken at Yankee Stadium, of all places; in the news clip, he said, "I am a Yankee!" Ada flicked off the TV and grabbed the phone on the third ring.

On the other end of the line, Clay Junior was in mid-sentence: "...old man's heart." It took a few seconds for her older brother's voice to register. Usually, Clay's wife, Big Junie, was the one on the line.

"Clay?" she said. "What did you say?"

Her brother oozed annoyance at her for not understanding right away. Their father had had a heart attack. It hadn't killed him, but close enough. A neighbor saw him collapse while reaching for the paper on the front stoop.

"You better get yourself to the ER," Clay directed, the first-born who ran the show. "Somebody has to be there. I have a business meeting." She knew the meeting was probably a fabrication. Clay owned a GM dealership in South Charlotte with multiple salesmen and a general manager. Their younger brother, Foster, claimed Clay had a work schedule "as loose as the change in my pocket."

Ada had been dreading this call for years, but she had expected a different disease to get her father. His lungs were as dense as a coal miner's from years of inhaling lint at the cotton mill and smoking Camels. His barking cough commanded a room. After her mother passed, there was no one to chide him to watch his habit or take it to the back yard, and a pack and a half a day inched up to two and then more. He should have been dead years ago but he just kept on going, like her old Timex. Now in the late stage of emphysema, he had oxygen always at the ready.

But his *heart?* Well, Foster had noted after a recent visit that their father didn't seem to eat anything but biscuits and sausage for breakfast, and Bojangles fried chicken with biscuits for supper. "He calls it his heritage. Sounds more like heart-attack-age," her brother quipped. A poor joke, but she did laugh, and now the memory embarrassed her. What kind of Christian daughter was she, to be so cavalier about her father's health?

"Cam," she said, nudging her partner awake with some difficulty. "Honey, wake up."

Cam sat up stiffly and glanced at the alarm. "Lord, darlin', did you forget it's June?" During the school year, they would have both been up and showered by now, but in the summer, Cam slept till eight.

"Clay Senior went and had himself a heart attack," Ada said. "I have to get to the hospital." She threw on clean clothes and ran a brush through her hair before hiding it under a bandana. At the last moment, she splashed some Jean Naté on her neck and arms—"a whore's bath," Granny Shook used to call it.

"I'll come with you."

Ada pretended to be preoccupied with locating her pocketbook and car keys. She didn't want to have to explain Cam's presence to anyone at the hospital. Suppose the ER staff didn't like gay people—would her father still get good care?

"Thanks, honey, but you stay and hold down the fort," Ada said at last. "I only woke you so you wouldn't worry. I'll try to call from the hospital and let you know what's what."

§ § §

She found her father in a faded hospital gown, hoses and instruments attached to various parts of his body. His closed eyelids and cracked lips had a faint blue tinge, matching the gown. "Death warmed over," one of her mother's many sayings, popped into her head.

Ada hadn't seen him since Christmas Day, when she traveled the five miles that separated them to bring him a poinsettia to brighten up the house. Every month after that she told herself she would visit him, take him a ham, give the place a good cleaning, but the calendar pages kept on flipping until it was June and he was lying on a gurney. She wanted to reach out and pet his hand, but they'd never had that kind of relationship.

"Hey, Daddy," she said several times, until his eyes popped open. A coughing jag was his first response.

"Sugar, your old man's falling apart."

"Oh, you'll outlive us all," Ada said.

"You here to spring me?"

"Daddy, you had a heart attack. A big one. You're not going home for a while." Her stomach listed at the thought that he wouldn't be able to take care of himself when it *was* time to go home. Ada had no reason to think Clay Junior or Foster would step up to the plate, or that their wives would allow it, for that matter—Big Junie and Bobbie Ann were daughters, too, and their own folks were getting on.

It was too early to start worrying, but Ada fretted just the same. She thought about Georgia, a colleague at school whose life had flip-flopped when her mother's dementia got so bad she set the kitchen curtains on fire. One day, Georgia and her husband were enjoying their empty nest, sharing snapshots of their train trip across Canada. The next, she was retiring early to become a full-time caretaker. "I'm the only girl," she had said at her going-away shindig, as if that were explanation enough.

§ § §

"You will not," Cam said, a week later, putting down her fork and refusing to eat any more of the blueberry pancakes Ada had made, special. "It doesn't have to be you. Foster's closer to him. Clay's the oldest. They've both got big houses to take him in. Hell, you don't even *like* him."

That last bit stung, but only because it was true. Ada was grateful her father had never skipped out on his family, or taken up with a younger woman, or drunk up his paycheck. She had smarted from his slaps, but he'd never crept into her room at night or touched her in an improper way, or slammed her into walls like he had her brothers.

Still, there wasn't much to like about him. She and Foster called him Archie Bunker behind his back. Somewhere along the way, her mother had stopped chiding him for using the N-word and it still popped up in his speech from time to time. "He was raised that way," her mother told Ada years back. "That's what folks said in the country. He doesn't mean it as hateful as you think."

Then there was his haranguing of her mother. "Will you just shut your trap?" he would say, often with an F-bomb for accent. "You are so damn stupid, woman." Ada couldn't imagine any Christian saying that to another, least of all the mother of his children.

And she didn't like that he had tried to stand in the way of her having a career until her mother intervened. "College isn't going to cost you a red cent," her mother said. "The girl won herself a scholarship, Clay."

"That ain't gonna help her find a husband," her father complained. "Librarians aren't nothin' but old maids with too much schooling."

Her mother rationalized that Ada's husband might die, or be maimed, or abandon her—all things that had befallen women in their mill community. A librarian was a solid job, one she could use if she needed to. "If something had happened to you while these children were growing up, well, we would have been on the dole for sure." *Dole* was a dirty word for Clay Senior, and that was enough to convince him a college-educated daughter was not so bad.

"He's a good man, when you dig down," her mother reminded her. *How far down do you have to go?* Ada wondered.

But she had to weigh more than just her feelings about him. Her mother had raised her to bring casseroles to the sick, even virtual strangers; it went without saying that you would do much, much more for kin, especially parents. *Honor thy father and thy mother.* How much easier it would have been if her mother had needed the tending instead of her father, but she had slipped away fast and early, at just sixty.

"Let him hire a nurse," Cam continued, picking at her pancakes.

"There's not enough money, even if the boys help out." In the pause that followed, the only sound was forks on plates. "He's offered to leave me the house, free and clear, if I stay with him and take care of . . . things. I guess I'll have to hire a lawyer to do it all legally, but we could come through this with a *house*, honey."

Cam grunted. The old bungalow was no prize, and Ada knew it. North Charlotte had deteriorated in the past twenty years: Yards that had once been pristine were now overgrown, businesses along the main drag were shuttered, drug deals occurred in the open, and even the theater where Ada and Cam once enjoyed movie dates had been triple X for years. Cam made it clear she worried every time Ada went to visit her father.

"I know what you're thinking," Ada said, because they'd lived together for almost thirty years and it was impossible not to know. "But the neighborhood's starting to turn around. People are getting federal money for renovations—that's what the neighbors told me. A *house*, Cam. No more renting. Aren't you thinking about retirement even a little?"

"I still have some stocks from my granny. It's not a fortune, but it'll help."

"And what about me?"

"It's *our* money, darlin'."

"And if something happens to you, nobody's going to see it that way."

"Nothing's going to happen to me."

"Well, I knew you were almighty, but I didn't know you were immortal, too."

Cam's face flushed, her objections cut off. They had gay male friends who were getting wills drawn up to avoid losing everything if their lovers died of AIDS. But the process had cost Twig and his lover Jimmy almost a thousand dollars. Having a little real estate of her own, Ada argued, would help settle her mind the same way a will would.

"And what am I supposed to do while you're off being his nurse?"

"Doctor says with his lungs and heart, he doesn't have long," Ada said. "The summer at best. I'll be with him most days and sleep there at night, but I could still have supper with you."

Cam grunted and left the table.

§ § §

In the beginning, he was a better patient than Ada expected. He greeted her each morning with a yellowed smile and told her more than once how grateful he was when she brought him his coffee. "Don't know where I'd be without you, sugar," he said as he watched her switch out his oxygen tank. "Probably face down somewhere."

"You are the king of exaggeration," she said.

It was one of her mother's sayings. Living in her parents' house, waking up in the same lumpy bed she had slept in as a girl, brushing her teeth in the pockmarked bathroom sink, spouting her mother's old saws, made her feel like someone had pushed the rewind button on her life. At the same time, she looked older to herself than ever. Lines were coming at the corners of her mouth, and her neck had folds she didn't remember seeing in her own bathroom mirror.

"Your hair's goin' gray," her father pointed out when she was leaning down to retrieve a magazine he'd dropped.

"I'm fifty-five, Daddy. If I didn't have some gray hairs, now *that* would be news." Her words sounded as scratchy as she felt. "And I sure don't have as much gray as you," she added, to lighten things up. He laughed, but like her, his moods were on a pendulum, swinging to the dark side without warning.

"This chair hurts," he said, trying to get up. "Get me outta here." She could see the veins popping through his skin as he attempted to lift himself from the chair.

"Sit down, Daddy. You could fall, and then we'd have a right mess, wouldn't we?"

"I will get up if I want to!" The first few times they'd played this scene, she tried urging him back into his seat with a promise of some sweet tea, just the way he liked it. But his muscles still had life in them, and he slapped her away. "Jesus H. Christ, girl, let me be! I don't want any tea! I want to get out of this goddamn chair!" Without Ada's mother there to remind him what it meant to be Christian, his speech was riddled with curse words.

Mealtimes, he was picky as a teenager. He was partial to all the foods the dietitian at the hospital had stripped right out of his regimen: biscuits, milk gravy, eggs, sausage, fried chicken, macaroni and cheese, ice cream sundaes. The scoop of Cheerios with skim milk that she laid out for his breakfast often went soggy in the bowl. At supper, he pushed his steamed broccoli and rice around his plate, and complained that her baked chicken tasted like a rubber hose.

"You're trying to kill me," he accused her.

If I was really trying to kill you, she thought as she tossed his uneaten food, *you'd be dead.*

His cardiologist chastised her when she brought him in for his checkup. "It's good for him to lose a little weight," the doctor observed, "but not this fast or this much. If you don't want your father to die of malnutrition, you best learn to cook something healthy that he likes."

"So now you're not just his nurse but his personal chef, too?"

Cam said. "Darlin', you have got to rethink this whole 'good daughter' thing. Let him go to the state hospital if he doesn't like the way you do things."

"I wouldn't send a junkyard dog there," Ada said. "Your daddy had money for good care when he was sick. Mine doesn't."

So she checked cookbooks out of the public library—titles like *Better Homes and Gardens Eating Light, Fit for Life,* and *Fresh Ways with Chicken*—and skimmed them for ideas. She learned ways to lighten up cheesy recipes, how to make "fried" chicken in the oven, and craft egg-white omelets. There was even a dessert made with bananas and vanilla yogurt that bore a fair resemblance to the pudding he craved. And although her father rarely complimented her on the new dishes, at least he ate them.

"He looks pretty good," Cam remarked, surprised, when she dropped in one Sunday. "But beats me why you have to go out of your way to make everything so healthy. I mean, he's dying."

It was a good point: If she were dying, she'd probably want to subsist on peach ice cream and pecan pie. Her father had blockage in three coronary arteries and the cardiologist wasn't recommending surgery. "He's eighty-eight years old," the doctor said, and left it at that.

But still, she persisted. "If he's strong, he can sign the house papers," Ada said. She was working with a gay woman lawyer Twig had recommended, someone who had a sliding scale for "family." Honor thy father or not, she was going to have her house.

§ § §

Her father was forbidden his smokes, and he seemed to have hidden them all over the house. Ada found everything from full packs to stray Camels tucked between the sofa cushions, under the mattress, in his sock drawer. The contraband went into the trash while he wasn't looking. Later, she'd spy him tugging at the edges of his mattress or rooting through a low cabinet, cursing softly.

"Remember what the doctor said. No smoking," she chided him when she discovered him with a cigarette she hadn't gotten to first.

"What harm's one little smoke gonna do now?"

"Well, for one, it'll blow us up to heaven," she said, nodding toward his portable oxygen. "And I'm not ready to go."

One evening when she returned from supper, and more, with Cam ("How about a quickie?" Cam had coaxed, but it had stretched into an hour) her father wasn't in any of his usual places: in front of the TV, on the porch, on the toilet. His wheelchair was sitting empty on the screened back porch, and Ada could see drag marks across the dirt from his walker. The door of the tool shed was wide open, the walker parked just outside it.

That was one place she had not thought to look when she was on the hunt for cigarettes. The shed was *his* space. She hadn't set foot in it in over forty years, not since the day as a girl when she'd gone to fetch a wrench for him and found the photographs. Ada approached the shed with trepidation and poked her head through the door.

"You okay, Daddy?" she called, without really looking. A circle of light from a single work lamp illuminated the center of the space. She heard the dragging of his shoes across wood as he navigated around the workbench and into the light.

"Looks like you caught me, gal," he said. An unlit cigarette hung from his lips. He tucked something away in the pocket of his trousers.

"Can't believe you made it all the way out here on your own. That's what's called pure determination."

"You threw out all my smokes."

"Good thing you didn't fall." She helped him down the one deep step to the yard. "You hiding more Camels in your pocket there?"

"Nah," he said, clutching onto the walker, but she didn't believe him.

His secret was in the trash the next evening, covered in coffee grounds and scraps from supper. She recognized the envelope as if her first encounter with it had happened just days before, not decades. Ada lifted it out of the trash, brushed it off, and stood holding it gingerly by one corner.

The sound of wheels on linoleum made her drop the thing like a hot skillet. It fell to the floor between them, and her daddy stared at it first, then at her.

"What're you doing, Ada Jane?" He rarely called her, or anyone for that matter, by name. It was always *gal* or *sugar* for her, *son* or *buddy* for her brothers.

"I put that in there for a reason," he said, leaning forward to retrieve the soiled envelope. "It's trash, plain and simple."

"I know what it is, Daddy."

"You looked inside?" he asked, his eyes cast down like a child caught doing something he shouldn't.

"Not today. But . . . way back when I was a girl." She had only told two people about the discovery—when it happened, Miss Ruthie, the public librarian whom she idolized; and then many years later, Cam.

The acknowledgment brought his blazing eyes up to meet hers. "What were you doing in my tool box?"

"I used to fetch your tools, remember? When Clay Junior didn't want to help anymore."

"You were too young to see this," he said, slapping the envelope against his thigh.

The naked women or the lynched blacks? she wondered.

"I ain't a bigot," he said. "You never seen me treating the coloreds at the mill any different . . ." A coughing fit cut off his explanation.

Ada brought him a glass of water, which he dismissed with a scowl. He slid the postcard of the lynching from the envelope and examined it, his fingers tracing the worn edges.

"My Uncle Rupert give this to me," he said. "My daddy's youngest brother. I was five, I reckon, maybe younger. That's me, right there." He pointed at a blurry figure in the foreground, one of several small children who appeared to be scooting past a tree where three blacks had been lynched. The men's bodies didn't even look human anymore. "Folks acted like the carny'd come to town. I didn't know no better, so I went along. But it seemed right gruesome to get your photo taken with some dead coloreds, so me and your aunt Nan—that's her—was trying to get away."

"But you didn't have to keep it," she said, her voice so hoarse she had to sip the water he had refused. "Why didn't you just throw it out?"

"Oh, I don't know," he said, acting peeved, as if he'd never cared to think about it. He tucked the photo into the envelope again. "Rupert got hit by a train a few years later. Out walking on the tracks after midnight, drunk as a skunk. He liked to take me places, like I was his kid brother." *What a show of affection*, she thought, taking a child to a lynching, but Ada held her tongue.

Her father thumbed through the other postcards in the envelope. "The rest of these pictures . . ."—he pronounced it *pitchers*—". . . hell, that's just stuff boys like to look at." He shot her a look she couldn't read. "Some girls, too, I reckon."

Ada's hands felt sweaty in the pockets of her dungarees, and she forced herself to hold one out for the envelope.

"You want that in the trash, then?"

"That's where I put it, ain't it?" His chair squealed a little as he turned.

That night, after she helped him to bed, the scene in the kitchen played in her head like a skipping record. She should have left the photos in the trash; she should never have asked him why he'd kept them. It would be just like the old man to spite her and call off the trip to the lawyer later that week. And why had he added that remark about women who liked to look at dirty pictures? She hadn't acknowledged her relationship with Cam to anybody in the family but Foster, and then only because he had guessed.

Ada lay awake reading, but kept losing her place and having to start whole paragraphs over. Around eleven, Cam phoned. She'd gotten her five-year chip from AA that evening and was all rambunctious energy, monologuing in double-time about the meeting. Later, she'd gone with AA buddies for ice cream sundaes. "I just love those folks!" she said.

Ada was quiet on the other end, her feelings morphing into rage. She needed to talk about what had happened with her father, but she couldn't get a word in.

"Sorry I'm rambling, darlin'," Cam said into the silence. "Must be on a sugar high."

She didn't mean to say it, but the thought jumped out anyway. "Sounds like a drunk high to me."

Cam took a couple of audible breaths. "I just got my chip, Ada Jane. I am going to pretend you didn't say that."

Ada was about to retract the remark and explain what happened with her father, but across the hall, the old man sounded like he was coughing up a lung. "I have to go," she said, but Cam hung up before she could explain.

The bloody phlegm was what made her call emergency services. "He's really sick," she explained. "Please hurry." She stood over him until they arrived, every prayer she had ever memorized coming to her lips.

§ § §

The next morning, Ada lugged her suitcase up the flight of stairs to their apartment and fumbled with the key. Cam was standing on the other side of the door looking like someone who had seen too many scary movies. In one hand she held a steaming mug of coffee while in the other she brandished her Swiss army knife, the long blade and corkscrew extended in Ada's direction.

"Sweet Jesus, what are you doing here?"

"I still live here, far as I know," Ada said, plopping her bag down just inside the door. To take the sting out, she quipped, "Were you going to scald me to death, or just corkscrew me?"

"Is he . . . ?"

Ada shook her head. "Admitted to the hospital. Last night. That's why I had to get off the phone so quick. Looks like pneumonia."

The three feet between them was a chasm Ada needed to

bridge. She went to Cam, took her mug, and set it down so she could hug her.

"I am so sorry," she said. "I was going to say so last night, but the old man started coughing like you wouldn't believe. I thought he was going to die on me right then and there." Cam usually welcomed hugs, could be almost greedy about them, but she remained stiff in Ada's arms, as if unready to forgive.

"Can I see your chip?"

"It's around, somewhere." Cam pulled away.

"Honey, I said I'm sorry. You had a great evening, and I had a rotten one. I took it out on you. Please forgive me."

"You were the one who asked me to stop drinking," Cam said, as if she'd quit immediately and not two years after Ada made the request. "And I did it, hard as it was, because you are the single most important thing in my life and I was afraid I'd lose you. I could never face that." She reached into the pocket of her cotton robe, withdrew the chip and held it out to Ada. "Then you go and slap me down. I did this for *you*, darlin'."

"Honey, you did it for yourself," Ada said. She turned the chip over and over in the palm of her hand, feeling its satisfying heft. *To Thine Own Self Be True* was stamped above the Roman numeral *V*.

"Bronze," Cam pointed out, and Ada nodded. Their eyes met as she slid it gently back into Cam's pocket.

§ § §

Clay Shook Senior passed two days later. This time the call came directly to her. "I understand. Yes. Thank you," she heard herself saying dully, as if on autopilot.

The death certificate read pneumonia, but the doctor targeted emphysema as the root cause. "His lungs got him in the end, no matter how you look at it," was how Ada delivered the news to both Clay Junior and Foster.

The trip to the lawyer never happened, so the house was lost to her. What would happen to it, without a will or any other paperwork? "Good thing you believe in eternal life," Cam said. "You'll be rewarded in heaven for being the good daughter, even if you didn't get the house."

Ada blinked back tears. Heaven was small comfort. Would she even see him there, a man who didn't recognize his own sins? Yes, she had wanted the house. But she'd wanted something less tangible, too, something a man like her father couldn't give.

Foster told her about the will when they were climbing back up the hill from their parents' graves. Clay Junior was farther ahead with Big Junie and their daughter, exchanging words with the preacher, while Cam walked with Foster's wife, Bobbie Ann, and their boys. Unaccustomed to wearing heels after a summer in flip-flops, Ada tripped and grabbed a hold of Foster's arm.

He said he had typed it for their father a year earlier, relying on a template from a how-to book, then drove him to have the thing notarized. Foster kept the original in his safe deposit box in Charleston. "He didn't want me to tell you or Clay," her brother said. "I have the dubious honor of being his executor."

"He let me plan the whole lawyer trip, but he had already made up his mind?" She had a stream of unchristian thoughts she kept to herself. "Tell me now, Foss—just get it over with. He left the house to Clay, didn't he?"

"I shouldn't tell you before we've officially read the thing, but he left you the house, big sister. Not that it's worth a hell of a lot. It'll be more a burden than anything else, unless you actually live in it."

Ada stared at her brother, her lips parted, unable to form words.

"He said we both had houses, but you didn't," Foster continued. "Said you didn't have a husband and could use the help."

He's a good man, when you dig down.

Days later, when she was sorting through her father's things, bagging up a donation for Goodwill, Ada found a baseball mounted on a polished wooden base. It had once sat on the mantle in the living room of their house, but at some point had migrated to a shelf in the closet. "Your daddy played for the

Carolina League 'fore I met him," her mother said when Ada was old enough to be curious about the ball. "The Mercury Mill boys. Scored the winning home run against High Point in the '24 finals."

"He didn't!"

"Yes indeed, missy. He's too humble to talk about it, but he could have been another Shoeless Joe if he hadn't hurt his hand at the mill the next year."

She didn't know who Shoeless Joe was, but the way her mother said the name made him sound important. Ada took to sitting on the screened porch with a fat book when her daddy was throwing pitches to Clay Junior in the back yard. She sneaked looks at him like he was a stranger, somebody else's father, encouraging his oldest son with "Attaboy" and "That one tricked ya, didn't it, son?"

Once and only once, after Clay had abandoned the bat and gone inside, her daddy had called out to her, "Gal, you want to take a swing?" Ada was graceless when it came to sports, always the last picked for teams, and she worried she might spoil her daddy's good mood. So instead of admitting, "I don't think I'd be any good at it, Daddy," she said, "I'm busy," and shoved her nose back into her book.

The memory reran in her head now, along with one of the last clear things he'd said to her: *Some girls, too, I reckon.* He'd said it with a sharp glance that made her wonder. In his own way, maybe he was just trying to tell her he knew her secrets as well as she knew his.

Eclipse

2003

Ada

"There's going to be a lunar eclipse November 9th," Cam said. "You can see it at 1:19, paper says."

Ada turned from the counter and placed a plate of scrambled eggs and grits on the table in front of Cam. "Don't you get any ideas."

Cam calculated with her fingers. "Eight days from today. I should be feeling okay. Maybe we could invite a few folks over?" In years past, they had always stayed up, and had even hosted a few eclipse-watching parties for their circle of friends.

"We'll talk about it. Just eat now. Twig'll be here any minute."

She watched until Cam picked up her fork and took a first bite, then a second. Nausea always ruled the first days after treatment, and Cam could only keep the blandest foods down. Her stomach stabilized by the end of the week, and Ada immediately set out to fatten her up with her favorite meals. Still, Cam had to use a plastic fork so the food didn't taste like it came from the scrap metal yard. In weeks two and three, she could eat with something resembling her usual gusto. And then it was back to square one. Today was the final round of chemo following her recurrence—unless her scan didn't look good and the doctor ordered more rounds.

"It's the first lunar eclipse of the century," Cam said as Ada plopped down across from her with a cup of coffee. "Seems like it calls for something. Want some grits, darlin'?"

Ada waved the food off, disgusted by the idea of it. She forced herself to make meals for Cam, although she herself had no appetite and had lost weight, too; her heart-shaped face was now chiseled to a point. Their friend Shirley Ann, a retired obstetric nurse, gave a name to her sympathetic nausea: "It's like Couvade syndrome. That's when a woman's pregnant, and her husband feels the symptoms."

Cam nudged her plate toward Ada. "Come on, have a bite. You got to stay strong so you can push my wheelchair around."

"You're not in a wheelchair."

"Not yet." Cam held the paper out, showing the progressive photographs of what a lunar eclipse looked like. "Wonder if it'll be one of those blood moons. This could be my last."

"Don't say that."

"Well, it could be your last, too. We just never know what's down the road."

Cam closed the paper and turned her full attention to her meal. "These grits are so silky it's like I don't even have to chew," she said.

Ada drained her cup and fetched the carafe; she needed not to look at the grits.

"You think I could have some, just half a cup?" Cam asked. "Green tea doesn't do it for me."

Ada pulled out a mug with a perfect red apple and *World's Best Teacher* printed on the side. They'd had it for years, along with an assortment of appreciative gifts from Cam's students, a veritable "who's who" of folks who had first read *To Kill a Mockingbird* and *A Raisin in the Sun* in her English classes. There were two men who were now in the state legislature, a woman who'd penned a hit song in the '80s, the mayor of a small town in eastern North Carolina, a best-selling mystery writer, a prominent Charlotte banker, the dean at a historically black college. Until she got sick, Cam had answered letters and emails from quite a few.

"The article I read said you need three or four cups of green tea a day for it to work."

"What's it do?" Cam said, finishing her plate.

"I don't know. Halts the cancer, shrinks the tumors. Something good. I'm not a doctor." As she poured the coffee, Ada splashed a puddle of liquid from the carafe onto the table, and she snapped at no one in particular: "Dang!"

"Darlin', it's okay," Cam said.

Ada rubbed the dishcloth over her mother's old maple table, again and again, until there were no traces of coffee and the wood shone.

"Sounds like Twig's out front," she said.

Their closest friend didn't have to knock. Ada heard the screen door slam behind him and then his long strides toward the kitchen, where he filled the doorframe with his height.

"Morning, ladies," he said. "Nice hat." The baseball cap, one of the many Cam owned and wore to keep her bald pate warm, featured a white palmetto tree and crescent moon on an indigo field—the South Carolina flag, a present from Foster.

"Have a seat, Twig, grab some coffee," Cam said. "Say, would you come if we have an eclipse get-together? November 9th."

"Don't know as I'm doing anything else."

"You two should get going, in case there's traffic," Ada said.

"What're you going to do with your free time?" Twig asked Ada when Cam went to the closet to fetch her jacket.

"Errands," she said immediately. "Nothing exciting at all." She'd practiced the casualness of her response in the bathroom mirror; she didn't want either of them to guess her actual plans.

"'Errands,'" Cam said, with a roll of her eyes. "That's probably code for a secret lover."

Cam

"You look right smart in that cap," Bettina said with a wink.

"I'm looking forward to the day when I don't have to wear it," Cam replied.

The chemo nurse was brawny, with power in her brown arms, enough to lift women too sick to do it themselves. Cam envied the ripple of her muscles. She was well over forty, but she wore no wedding band and never mentioned children or grandbabies; never mentioned anybody, really. She kept her nails and hair short, unlike the other nurse, whose blonde ponytail bounced behind her and whose manicure looked like it could snag some patient's delicate skin. Cam recognized the telltale signs of being "in the life," but if she was a kindred spirit, Bettina had never let on.

"Hook me up, Bettina. Let's get this show on the road."

It was a small room, and Twig had to wait elsewhere for Cam for the five hours of treatment. "Don't you have too much fun," Cam said, "or I'll be jealous."

"I'll just find me a coffee shop."

After the initial dose of Benadryl slithered into her system, Cam fell into a blissful grogginess in which the other voices in the room were just background noise that carried her off to sleep. She had always been an easy sleeper, and she particularly welcomed it during chemo. The matrons in the room weren't much for talking, except about husbands and children. Often, they swapped recipes of easy meals they could make their families in the months they were undergoing treatment. "My husband's pretty tired of getting takeout from Bojangles!" one woman laughed.

"Why doesn't he cook for you, then?" Cam had asked aloud, making all heads turn to her in speechless surprise. Only Bettina let a faint smile cross her lips.

After her peaceful snooze, the final round was over and Cam was the only patient left in the room. Bettina disengaged the IV from her port with her usual skill.

"I'll miss seeing you, Bettina," Cam said. "You are something special, truly. One damn fine nurse."

"Well, you might . . ." Bettina began but bit off the end of her thought. *Be back,* was what shot through Cam's mind.

". . . stop in the next time you're seeing Dr. Tartt," Bettina concluded. "I love getting a report on all my ladies."

"You watch out. I just might do that."

Twig had observed the exchange from the doorway. "Honey,

I've seen everything now," he said. "Were you just flirting with the chemo nurse? I might have to tell Ada."

"You think she doesn't know me by now?"

Twig was supposed to bring her directly home, but the sky was such a deep shade of blue it felt like high summer, and Cam wheedled and cajoled until he took a side excursion to Pike's Soda Shop. "You can't deny a dying woman's wish for a chocolate shake on a beautiful day, now can you?"

"Ah, you ain't dying."

They perched on stools at the counter, even though she felt almost too tired to hold herself up straight. She loved to see the fountain ware lined up so neat and precise, to watch the soda jerks assemble sundaes and banana splits right in front of her.

"My one and only job in high school was at the Soda Shop in Davidson," she said. "I ever tell you that?"

"You may have. Don't recall."

"My mama didn't think girls should work, but Daddy was proud that I was making my own spending money. The shop opened that year and I got hired for the summer, before going off to Greensboro. I came home smelling like sugar every damn day. Just about ruined my love of treats. I didn't touch ice cream or Coke all through college."

She stopped the soda jerk as he was reaching over to serve her shake. "Do me a favor, hon, and top it off with a little whipped cream, would you?"

Twig picked at his hot fudge sundae like he was on a diet, while she sucked her shake with appreciation.

"God, girl, you are making a racket."

"I won't feel like eating again for days," she said. "Have to savor it while I can. What's with you and that sundae?"

"I'm worried Ada's gonna have my hide," Twig said, pushing the dish away. "We should go soon."

"We'll tell her we stopped for green tea." But the joke tasted sour, even to Cam, and her old friend's face clouded with discomfort. He brushed a shock of white hair out of his eyes. She cherished just looking at him, loved how they'd grown old knowing each other and that he'd stuck around even for the bad parts. Cam had come to expect that loyalty from her tight group of friends, to count on it and give it in return like the comfort it was. "Gay folks need each other" were the words she lived by.

So it smarted that her friend Lu had made herself scarce. Lu had been faithful at first; she was with Cam the day she collapsed, with so much internal bleeding she almost died. Lu called 911 and stayed at the hospital for hours with Ada, waiting for word. And she stuck around through surgery and the first treatments, even paying for a woman to clean their house on a regular basis.

When the cancer recurred, though, Lu vanished like Cam was already in the ground and the job of friend was done. "I am just so *busy*," she said, when Cam invited her to supper during a good week. "I'll have to take a rain check." But she never followed up, and messages left on her answering machine went unreturned until Cam simply stopped calling.

"Busy my behind," Twig had snapped, but even his fierce devotion couldn't take away the sting of Lu's rejection. Cam hadn't known anyone as long as Lu, not even Ada. Lu had been a pain in the ass more than once, with her diva ways and a jealousy of Ada that still flared. And yet, Cam had taken it for granted she would always be there.

Cam finished her shake and reached for a spoonful of Twig's hot fudge. After, she left a chocolatey imprint of her mouth on her thin paper napkin and then let out a deep, satisfied sigh. "Thank you for this, my friend. I feel almost normal."

"I do miss us being normal," Twig sighed.

She knew he meant more than just the two of them eating ice cream. Twig had nursed his lover Jimmy through AIDS and still lived with the scar tissue and survivor guilt. When he visited Cam for the first time after her diagnosis, he had tried to joke casually, but later told Ada he got into a fender-bender on his drive home.

His eyes were wet now, so Cam jumped in to make him laugh again. She had never done well with weepy, and less so now that the tears were about her. "Oh, honey, normal is one thing we will *never* be."

Ada

On the front porch, a plump pumpkin sat surrounded by an assortment of much smaller gourds, like a mother hen overseeing her chicks. A wreath crafted from artificial sunflowers, autumn leaves, berries, and miniature pumpkins hung on the door, with a pair of felt Pilgrim dolls affixed to the top like a bow.

The fall colors complemented the forest green trim of the townhouse to perfection, and at any other time, Ada would have commended Lu on her seasonal decorations, which she likely had crafted herself. But all Ada could think as she pressed the doorbell twice, then once more for emphasis, was: *How dare she even* think *about decorating!*

Lu was at home, that much was clear; her smart little Kia was parked at the curb. It was too late in the morning to be taking a shower, even for Lu. Ada poked at the bell another three times, then stepped off the porch and glared up at the second-floor windows. There was no sign of movement within. Ada had just turned back to her car, unkind thoughts crowding her mind, when the front door opened.

"You don't give a lady much of a chance to get to the door, Ada Jane," Lu said. "I was all the way upstairs in the bathroom, and you just kept ringing and ringing. I don't get around as well as I used to, you know. I thought it was the Jehovah's Witnesses come to harass me."

The word *harass*, with its slight emphasis, wounded her, but Ada didn't let on. Though Cam's college roommate had grown on her over the years, Ada could still be cowed by the woman's barbs. Not today, though. "I don't know any such thing. Shirley Ann said she ran into you last week coming back from playing nine holes. Sounds to me like you get around just fine."

"Oh, Shirley Ann," Lu said, as if her ex were the biggest liar she'd ever known.

Ada raised an eyebrow. "May I come in?"

The living room looked as pristine as always, as if no one ever used it. Lu still had the resources to have a woman come in every other week. "The place is a mess," she said, "so promise you won't tell. It's Maribel's week off."

"Who would I tell?" Ada snapped. A look of shock crossed Lu's face, as if she feared the worst—that Cam had passed and Ada had come to inform her. "You know Cam doesn't care about such things, and I rarely see anyone else these days but Twig."

"Twig comes around?"

"At least once a week, sometimes twice. To visit with Cam or take her out. He took her to her last chemo today."

"So she's . . . all right, I take it," Lu said. "If chemo's over."

"No, she's not 'all right,' Lu. The doctor hasn't given us much hope this time around." Ada felt her eyes welling up, but she hadn't come for Lu's pity. They were standing in the middle of the room, as immobile as pieces of furniture, and Lu was curling and releasing her fingers in an anxious way.

"Well, I didn't mean that she's cured or anything, of course," Lu backtracked. "I just meant . . ."

"Do you mind if I sit?" When Lu motioned toward the sofa, Ada sank into it, her jacket still on, pocketbook in her lap. "The thing is, how would you know if she's 'cured or anything'? You never call. You never come 'round." Her anger at Lu exhausted her, but she pushed on just the same. "You abandoned her when she needed you most. Like you dropped off the face of the earth. She would never have done that to you."

"Oh, don't go on like that!" Lu laughed, a nervous little twitter. "You've known exactly where I am. Why, here you are, sitting in my living room."

Ada had never slapped anybody in her life, but now she imagined herself leaving a red handprint on Lu's powdered cheek. She could almost hear the satisfying crack of it. As if she could read Ada's thoughts, Lu's eyes opened wide.

"That was unkind of me," Lu said. "I apologize."

"It was a mistake to come," Ada said, standing up.

"No, it wasn't. Please. I have some pastries. I'll make tea."

"I don't want anything." Ada took her seat again, but she couldn't look directly at Lu. Instead, her eyes fell on the coffee table, on the latest issues of *Ladies Home Journal* and *Martha Stewart Living*.

"Well, I feel like I should give you *something*. It's an occasion. You have never visited me without Cam before, not in forty-odd years. Why, we won't even be friends anymore if . . ." The words quivered out of her and landed in the space between them.

Ada looked up and scanned Lu's face. With her carefully styled bob and violet eye shadow, she was still attractive but a bit too much. Only Lu would make herself up like that—and at home, no less—or have her hair dyed raven black, as if she fancied herself forty instead of seventy.

Her sudden vulnerability was hard to ignore, though. Ada had seen it before. Twenty-some years back, Lu's mother had succumbed to breast cancer after what her obituary called "a brief but valiant struggle." Ada's own mother had died of breast cancer a few years before Lu's, in a whoosh of a death that left her daughter breathless and unmoored. "There's nothing so wrenching as the death of your mama," Ada had said at the time to comfort her, and Lu had yielded to her hug—the only occasion on which they'd ever really touched.

Remembering that exchange made something soften inside Ada. She felt a pinch of sadness for Lu, all alone in her pristine house. "Oh, we'll still be friends, Lu," she offered, though she couldn't say the words *if Cam passes*. "Cam would want that. But what *I* want is for you to be a friend to her right now."

Her anger came sputtering back with Lu's next words. "I don't need pity, thank you, Ada Jane. And I don't need you telling me how to be friends with Cam. I've known her longer than you. But maybe you begrudge me that. Or maybe you can't stand it I had that one time with her. I mean, honestly—she did choose you."

131

Ada's mouth popped open, and Lu's hand flew up to her cheek. "Oh, Lord, honey, I just assumed you knew. I mean, all those years you've been together . . ."

Recovering her composure as quickly as she could, Ada tensed her lips so they wouldn't open again on their own. "Of course I knew. There's nothing I don't know about Camellia Lively, believe you me."

Even as she said it, she felt a stitch in her heart, like a splinter had settled in and wouldn't work loose. Not because Cam had lied about Lu so long ago, but because she couldn't help speculating about what other lies and omissions there had been over the years.

Ada stood again to go, this time for sure, wanting nothing more than to be on the other side of the door. She took her time getting there, though, even letting a few rote civilities pass her lips: "You take care" and "Give Cam a call some time." She had intended to tell Lu about the tentative plans for an eclipse get-together, but she knew now she would never invite Lu to her house again.

She meant to go home or to the grocery store, but the car took her instead to the boulevard where Cam had lived when they met, where Ada had moved in and they'd lived together for almost thirty years. Tall potted plants obscured the balcony of their former second-floor apartment, but other than that, the place still looked remarkably the same. It was not a part of town she frequented anymore, and Ada sat for a few minutes with the motor running.

The lipstick, she thought. All those years ago, before they were lovers, Cam had held a book club at her apartment and, despite everything Ada had ever learned about good manners, she had snooped in the medicine cabinet. Sitting alone on a glass shelf was a tube of lipstick, a shade of coral she could picture Lu wearing. Later, Ada asked Cam if she had been involved with Lu romantically, but she denied it, and the tube was gone by the time Ada spent her first night there.

The suspicion had collected dust in Ada's mind just the same.

132

Now, Cam was sick; it would be cruel to have it out with her. Ada would have to force herself to stay buttoned up, to try not to stare at Cam and wonder.

Cam

Ada's Buick wasn't in the carport when Twig pulled up to the bungalow. Cam was not one to worry, but panic tugged at her just the same. Ada had invited Twig to supper, and it was just after four, so where was she?

"She doesn't have a cell phone, does she?"

"Doesn't believe in them," Cam said. "Maybe she got out of the house later than she expected. I guess I won't worry yet. She probably left us a note."

There was no note, but the phone was ringing as Cam unlocked the door. Twig hovered anxiously next to her as she answered it. The voice on the other end was a shock, but Cam greeted the caller with equal parts forgiveness and glee. "Well, if it isn't Miss Lu Pardue! Where have you been, girl?"

But after a quick apology for jumping ship on her, Lu steered right to the point.

"Oh, hell, Lu," Cam said. "Why'd you go and do that? I mean, we were never going to be anything, you and me. If you still think after all these years that Ada came between us, well, that's flat-out wrong." Lu sputtered some apologies that Cam couldn't hear through a drumming in her ears. "Look, just don't bother calling here again."

"Shit," Twig said when she hung up and told him. "I can't believe you never told her about you and Lu."

"I didn't see the point. It was just that one night. I was drunk and out of my mind about Viv breaking up with me. Lu wanted something more, she pressured me about it, but then I met Ada and that was that. And I thought Ada would be uncomfortable with me and Lu being friends if she knew."

"Should I drive around and look for her?"

"She's mad, that's all. She's cooling off."

Twig opted to go home so they could have private time when Ada did return. Cam waited for her at the kitchen table, trying to read the paper but actually listening for the sound of her steps on the front porch. Maybe the wait was her punishment for everything—drinking too much all those years ago, keeping an ex-lover as a friend, getting cancer, not once but twice.

The sun had faded when she finally heard Ada's key in the lock, but Cam didn't get up to turn on the light. From the front room, there was no "Hon, I'm back," just the sounds of Ada hanging up her coat in the closet and a big sigh. Cam watched Ada move across the room, in and out of her line of vision, then finally turn toward the kitchen with two bags of groceries from Food Lion.

"Why are you sitting in the dark?" Ada asked, flipping on the bright overhead.

"Too lazy to get up."

Ada eyed Cam with suspicion, then began opening and closing cabinet doors noisily as she put her purchases away. "Did chemo go okay?" When there was no response, she moved to the refrigerator and chucked the fresh vegetables into the crispers, as if they had been bothering her. "And where's Twig? Didn't he want supper after all?"

"He wanted to give us some time alone. Guess who called just a little while ago."

Ada stopped what she was doing but didn't turn around. "Who?"

"I think you might be able to guess."

Ada ran a hand through her hair and slowly faced her. "I went there to see why she left you high and dry," she explained. "I've been seething at her, and I thought I'd just have it out. So imagine my surprise when she springs *that* on me. I was mortified, completely humiliated. I could hardly see straight to drive. I didn't deserve that, Cam."

"Lu's the one who should be mortified," Cam said. "It's just sick that she would tell you such a thing after all these years."

"She must still love you."

Cam waved off the suggestion, not caring if it was true or not. "That's her problem," Cam said. "I chose you."

Ada moved to the table and sat down, her forehead lined with worry. "I know you did, and I would have never even brought the thing with Lu up, not now. But I do wonder what else you haven't told me. Or if this lie about Lu . . ."

"More an omission, I'd say."

". . . this omission about Lu is . . . well, I wonder if you're keeping more from me."

"This is the honest-to-God truth, Ada. It was just one time with Lu. She was furious with me for a while, but we got past it and mended our friendship. There were good memories with her worth saving, I thought. And I didn't want to dig it up again by telling you."

"So why . . ." Ada stopped and bit her bottom lip, but she clearly had something she needed to ask. "Why did you keep her lipstick?"

Cam fished around in her memory, but chemo had left its toll on her powers of recollection and she couldn't come up with anything about a tube of lipstick. "What lipstick?"

"The book club," Ada said. "The one you started because you wanted to get me to your apartment?"

"Yeah, I remember that."

"Well, I went to the bathroom while I was there—Lu was needling me, the way she has from day one, and I just needed to take a break. And I opened up your medicine cabinet and there was this single tube of lipstick. Which you never wore."

Cam's cheeks felt warm.

"Oh, no, darlin', no," she said sadly. She had to tell her; Ada had been with her through everything, truly in sickness and in health, watching her get thinner and frailer, holding her while she vomited into a bucket. The woman deserved an honest answer. "That was Viv's."

They hadn't spoken of Viv in twenty years. Ada was her love and her life, but Viv was the one who broke her heart.

"So it's always been Viv."

"Ada Jane . . ."

"I guess I'm not surprised. I mean, I was just the skinny little white girl who didn't care much about politics, and you and Viv were traipsing off to civil rights rallies together. I couldn't compete with a black woman in your eyes, could I? No wonder you went on a bender when you found out she got married. No wonder you acted so entranced when we ran into her in New York."

"Ada Jane," Cam said, slowly and in a measured tone, "I was foolish to keep that lipstick, but you know I am sentimental. Viv was really the first big love for me, and she hurt me bad. Now I don't have that lipstick anymore, and you won't stumble on it when I die. I tossed it out when you and I got together. There's nothing more being hidden from you."

Ada's forehead seemed to loosen and relax, like she wanted to believe her.

"The fact is, Viv did me a favor when she left me. If she hadn't, I might have missed the one I was meant to be with. I wish you could see yourself as I have all these years, your pluck, your resilience, that spark that shows up when you least expect it. You were a girl who wasn't even sure she was gay, but you swallowed all your fear and took a chance on us. I chose you, but you chose me right back."

She had wrapped her hands around Ada's as she spoke. Ada made a halfhearted attempt to free them, but then she gave in and Cam just held on tight.

Comfort Zone

2015

The day the old man showed up, the thermometer was already topping 80° by mid-morning. The trips carrying grocery bags from the trunk of the Buick Century to the front steps of her bungalow left Ada's light green shift saturated at the armpits. She regrouped after each one, catching her breath and readjusting the strap of her pocketbook, which kept slipping from her shoulder. The checkers at Food Lion didn't know how to pack anything properly, insisting on putting the cans and milk in one bag, even when she told them not to. Then they'd ask, "You need some help, ma'am?" *You gonna come home with me?* she wanted to snap.

With sweat tickling her breasts and plastering her white bob to her forehead, Ada eased her bones onto the bottom step of her porch with a whoosh of a sigh. And that was when she saw him, standing on the sidewalk not ten feet away, staring at her, round-mouthed and dim-looking in his "Property of Steelers" T-shirt. *His elevator doesn't go all the way to the top floor.* He had a few years on her, but the strength still visible in his forearms suggested he'd known a life of manual labor. What kind of man, especially one her own age who was still fit, would let a woman tussle with all those bags and never offer to carry even one?

"What're you looking at?" Ada knew better, she hadn't been raised like that, but still she couldn't help it—it just popped out of her mouth before she could stuff it back in, as if old age gave her permission to forgo the manners she'd learned as a girl.

He brushed his hair out of his eyes, which were a shade of blue that reminded Ada of the sky at Folly Beach. "Do you know me?" the old man asked.

"Don't recollect so," Ada replied, thinking it was the oddest question anyone had asked her since she retired as school librarian.

"Oh," he said, his chest sinking in a little.

She waited for him to say something else or to finally come to his senses and offer help getting the bags inside. But then, her niece Junie had cautioned her against letting anyone into the house; she'd read a story about scammers who targeted the elderly by claiming to be financial planners with the inside scoop on some great new mutual funds.

"They're mutually funding folks right out of their savings!" was how Junie put it.

This old man, though, didn't look like he had anything wicked in mind. Several years past eighty, he surely didn't mean to rape or murder her, or even steal her pocketbook. His clothes were clean and pressed, like someone was taking care of him, a wife, she guessed, by the thin gold band on his left hand. But he looked a little jumpy, the way he kept drifting from one foot to the other as he stared her down. Maybe he'd misplaced something important, like his keys or wallet or even his dog. People's dogs and cats were always going loose in the neighborhood and having to be rounded up. Somebody's orange tabby practically lived in her back yard.

"You lose something?" Ada decided to ask.

He looked up and down the street twice, three times, then back at Ada. "This your house?"

"Free and clear," Ada said. "My daddy left it to me." The five-room house with a screened back porch had been a bone of contention with her brother Clay until his dying day. "Would have been fairer to sell it and split the proceeds," he had complained, seeming to forget he owned a sprawling property on Lake Norman and didn't need the money.

"It's nice," the old man said. "Needs some work, though." He had no drawl, and must be a Northern transplant.

Ada took silent offense at his statement, even though what he said was true. Cam had been handy and had kept the place up, but she'd been gone almost a dozen years. The exterior hadn't had a coat of paint in that long, and a couple of floorboards on the front porch had rotted away like bad teeth. Some of the screens were so frayed, she might as well have put out a welcome mat for mosquitoes. More worrisome were the furnace and hot water heater—her daddy had installed them so long ago the date had slipped from her memory, and Ada prayed that they would make it through another year. With repairs, the place might be worth some money now. Newcomers were snapping up old cotton-mill houses all over the neighborhood. Two doors down, Mr. Barlow's sons had fixed up his tumbledown shotgun after he died and then turned around and sold it for well over $200,000—more money than Ada could even imagine.

But there was no time to chitchat with the old man about improvements to her house. At another time, she might have engaged, but in this heat Ada had to get her perishables inside. "I got to go," she said to the Steelers fan, and hauled herself up by the wrought iron banister which, she noticed with alarm, was starting to come loose from the steps.

"You know my daughter?" the old guy continued. "Mimi Finn?"

"Can't say I do."

"She's from Pittsburgh, like me," he went on. "I live with her and her . . ." He broke off. "I live with her. Right around here." He glanced around again, giving Ada the impression he was not quite clear on where "here" was. She wondered if she should help him out, but how long would that take? Sometimes, when you tried to assist people, be a good neighbor, you ended up taking on more than you bargained for, and Ada had concerns of her own. Getting old was no Sunday afternoon picnic, and she had the creaking joints and shrinking bank account to prove it. Luckily, she still had all her faculties.

"Family's what's important," she said, just to say something and have the exchange be over and done with. "You have a nice day." She adjusted her pocketbook again and mounted the steps

139

with one of the heavier grocery bags in tow. At this rate, her frozen chicken potpies would be thawed before she got through the front door.

"You want a hand?" the old man asked.

Ada remembered Junie's warning, but then, maybe her niece didn't have to know. Junie didn't check in more than once a week, so maybe it wasn't even any of her business. She was quick to tell Ada what not to do, but not so fast when it came to coming around for a glass of sweet tea or sending her son Matt to mow the lawn. Now Ada had an offer of help precisely when she needed it. "I'd be much obliged," she replied.

"I'm Harry. Harry Finn."

"Ada," she said. "What's your shirt mean?"

Harry looked down at it, as if he'd forgotten what he was wearing. "It means I'm from Pittsburgh," he said.

"Then shouldn't it say, 'I'm from Pittsburgh'?"

Harry's mouth fell into that rounded O again.

"It's a joke," Ada explained, and he laughed like kids did when they didn't want to seem foolish. "Here," she said, pointing to the heaviest two bags, the ones with canned beans and a bottle of Crisco oil that she worried might crack her spine like a piece of dry wood. "Bring those two inside. Please."

"Glad you added the please," Harry said, as he scooped up the bags and hauled them across the threshold. "I was wondering about that Southern hospitality I heard about." It was the longest thing he'd said to her in the five minutes of their acquaintance, and it was surprisingly clear as spring water.

She watched his eyes scan the genteel tatters of her living room. Ada kept it neat, but the wallpaper she and Cam had hung when they moved in was faded to grays and beiges and curling at the match lines. The sofa looked like you might sink through to China if you sat on it. "It's not much," she said, seeing it through a stranger's eyes. "Kitchen's right through here."

"Nice you got your own place."

She switched on the kitchen overhead and the fluorescent bulb flickered before going on full force. Ada placed her grocery bag on the table, set with a single placemat and chair, and motioned for Harry to do the same. He returned to the porch for the rest of the bags, his second trip taking a little longer than the first. The least she could do, she thought, was offer him some sweet tea, show him she *was* hospitable after all.

"Don't mind if I do," Harry replied.

"Sit yourself down in the other room. Take a load off."

She put away the frozen foods, milk, and eggs and poured him a tall glass on ice. As an afterthought, she pinched a sprig of mint from her windowsill herb garden and stuck it in his glass, where it stood up like a soldier at attention.

"What's that?" Harry asked, staring at the mint like it was a foreign object you'd never find in sweet tea—a dead bug, maybe.

"You never saw mint before?"

"Not like that," he replied.

"How else would you see it?" There was her ornery side again. She didn't mean to sound so clipped, but the guy was mighty peculiar.

"I like them York Peppermint Patties. My wife used to stick one in my lunch pail every so often."

He was sitting on the sofa, on the middle cushion, which was sturdier than the other two and made him rise up like a dignitary. Ada sat down across from him in her TV chair, the La-Z-Boy that had been her daddy's and that Cam had insisted they keep. Her shift made her descent more of a plop than a sit, because she worried that her hemline might hike up. She resisted the urge to make the chair recline, which would have added to the problem, even though she could feel her ankles swelling from all the standing she'd done while shopping. She would have to soak them in Epsom salt later.

"You and your wife live with your daughter?" she said, finding it surprisingly pleasant to have a guest, even one who didn't get her jokes.

Harry sipped the tea and murmured his approval. "No, just me. Sharon died." It was startling the way he came out with it, just like that. Ada still couldn't refer to Cam's passing, when she spoke of it at all, as anything but that—a temporary crossing until they met again on the other side. *May she rest in peace.*

"I am truly sorry to hear that," she replied. "What was it that got her?"

"Stroke. Doctor said she didn't feel a thing."

"Well, that's a blessing," Ada said. Cam's ovarian cancer had been ruthless, going away and then coming back. It was like an alien beast that'd been gestating inside her, waiting for the cruelest moment to show up, just when they had begun to live like regular folks again.

The images still haunted her—the chemo room drip, the "sick bucket," just in case, the sight of Cam curled up under an afghan on the couch all day, reduced to the weight of a girl. She'd been an imposing woman most of her life, six foot tall in her stocking feet, with the strong legs of an athlete. Ada tried to banish the sickroom Cam quickly so she didn't take root and keep her awake at night.

"Nice place you got here," the old man said, as if their preceding conversation had never taken place. "You own it?"

What could she say to that? At the senior center, which she went to a few afternoons a month for the free movies, there were plenty of folks like this man, their marbles slipping away one by one. She never knew what to say to them either, when they hopped on the same train of conversation they'd dropped out of, not minutes earlier. Ada was glad to still have her wits about her, but it was a lonely state of affairs, too.

Luckily, she didn't have to struggle with re-answering the old man's question. Just like the folks at the East Charlotte Senior Center, Harry's attention span seemed to be no longer than about five seconds. "Your husband dead?" he asked.

"No husband," she said. "I lived with a . . . friend. She's gone almost twelve years now."

Her eyes darted to a grouping of photos of Cam, given prime place on her mother's étagère. When Junie came to visit, Ada put the pictures away, replacing them with knickknacks she stashed in a drawer for that purpose. But she hadn't been expecting company. It was daring to have the photographs out, right in the open like that, but she hoped the old man's eyesight was as malfunctioning as his brain. Maybe he wouldn't notice that in one of them, a young Ada and Cam were sitting on the beach with their bare shoulders boldly touching, as if daring the world to see their intimacy. Auggie had snapped the picture and framed it, given it to Ada for Christmas as a memento of what he called a "*très* gay" weekend, probably back in '59 or '60. The year might have slipped from memory, but she would never forget the thrilling press of Cam's freckled skin against her own.

Harry's eyes followed her own to the shelves. "That her?" he said, taking a long swig of his sweet tea. "The friend?"

She dodged the question, even though a dim bulb like him would probably never put two and two together. "You got good eyesight, seeing that from where you're sitting. I'm useless without my glasses."

"I seen it when I was waiting for the tea," he commented. "Nice-looking woman. My wife would've called her 'a big girl.'"

Silence dropped between them again. If someone commented on the looks of your husband or child, you might say thank you, but what did you say about a nice-looking *friend*, a woman whose only connection to you now was memories? Ada shifted in her chair. She was ready for him to leave, but he went on.

"My daughter's got a friend. A woman. She gets mad if I use that word *friend*. She says *wife*. I didn't think it was right when she first told us, but times change and at least they take care of each other." The rattle of his ice cubes as he drank more tea echoed in Ada's ears. "You know my daughter, Mimi?"

This time it was Ada's mouth that dropped open. She had definitely had enough of the Steelers fan, coming out of nowhere and upending her day, acting like he knew something about her and Cam. She would put the photo of the beach away as soon as he left; their life together wasn't his business. They had never discussed their relationship in public, hardly even with their gay friends. And strangers? Shoot, Ada would have sooner told a stranger about her bowel movements than admit to having a special woman friend or, heavens, a *wife*.

Bile rose in her throat like it did when she ate too fast. Would Harry Finn start running off at the mouth about meeting an old gay gal who lived on her own? He was just demented enough to, not even realizing what he was doing, and she wouldn't want any hooligans finding out and deciding to bother her. The neighborhood had its share of crime, but so far she'd been spared and she wanted to keep it that way. Ada yanked herself out of the chair and came toward him, taking the glass from his hand. He relinquished it without protest, the tinkle of the unmelted ice like a chime ending his stay.

"I told you before, I don't know her," she said. "And fact is, I got chores to do now." A lame excuse—there was nothing whatsoever to do until supper, and then she would just zap a potpie in the microwave.

She knew she should have detained him, tried to figure out where his daughter lived. But some nasty version of Ada Shook whispered in her ear like the devil himself. She would have to pray on it later, ask God and Cam to forgive her.

At the front door, Harry looked up and down the street as if the terrain were Jupiter and not a quiet urban landscape. She had heard of the state's silver alerts, like the amber alerts for missing kids but for old folks, poor souls who couldn't find their way home even if they were just a street or two away. On the porch, as the screen door slapped behind him, the man turned back toward her and reached into his pants pocket. His eyes were dark and hooded, and she flinched, wondering if he was someone to fear after all. Why hadn't she noticed the bulge in his pocket?

But what he pulled out was a flip phone, the kind that you could send away for from *Parade* magazine. She had one, too, with numbers as big as her thumbnail and an old-fashioned ring like the phone that still hung on her kitchen wall. Junie had bought the thing for her but she had used it only once, when she came out of the senior center to a flat tire. The old man held his phone out to her. "Does this thing tell you where I live?" he asked with an embarrassed laugh, more of a snort. "Darned if I can figure it out."

She took it from him and stabbed the button for Contacts. There was just one—Mimi—but no address accompanied the phone number. The street might have been on there somewhere, but Ada wasn't sure how to find it. She should have pressed the number and called Mimi Finn herself, but instead she handed the phone back to him like it was a dead mouse.

"No address I can see."

"Oh," he said. "Well, thanks anyway." Then he turned, looked both ways on the street again, and stepped off the porch without a goodbye.

§ § §

"I never saw him before, that's the truth," she told the two young officers, one man and one woman, who showed up in the middle of her supper explaining that one of the neighbors had seen the old man go into her house. Now the police said he was missing.

They showed her a phone, which looked pretty much like the one he had asked her to check for his address. "Could be his," she admitted. "I only saw it for a second or two. He wasn't here but a short time." The male cop pressed her on what a "short time" was—was it as much as a half-hour? An hour?

"I don't know," she said, which was the truth. "It was . . . short."

The exchange made her ears warm to the touch. The police took notes and thanked her politely for the information, calling her "Mrs. Shook," and she didn't correct them. When they left, Ada threw out the rest of her chicken potpie, which had gone cold, and turned on the TV.

In the close discomfort of the living room, she adjusted the big box fan, aiming it so it blew the hem of her shift and sent a chill up her bare legs. *The People's Court* helped take her mind off the cops until she dozed off in her chair.

But her nap was fitful and far from refreshing. She dreamed that she found the old man collapsed on her couch, his glass of sweet tea spilling and soaking into the cushions. His skin was chill to the touch as she bent over him, saying, "Are you dead?" over and over. She was just inches from his face when his eyes popped open, and then she screamed and woke up.

§ § §

By morning, Ada had almost backed the old man into a far corner of her mind. She didn't think about him while she was getting dressed and putting on a pot of coffee, or even when she set out her Cheerios with sliced banana. But when she went out on the porch to get her newspaper, she was jolted back to the memory of him standing on the sidewalk, staring at her with those arresting eyes.

She pulled the paper from its plastic sleeve, but the front-page headlines held no clues about an old man's disappearance from the neighborhood. He'd surely been found by now, she thought. How far could he go? It was true, there was an old lady who had wandered off the year before and tumbled into Little Sugar Creek, hitting her head on a rock and drowning before anyone could locate her. But she was a fragile thing, hunched and bird-like. Ada had seen the photo in the paper. Harry Finn looked like he would survive a fall.

From the porch, Ada noticed that someone had posted a sign on her utility pole, and she stepped out to investigate. Her stomach did a belly dive as the old man's photo stared back at her from the pole. He was seated in front of a birthday cake, poised to blow out the candles. HAVE YOU SEEN MY FATHER? was printed in bold letters across the top. ANSWERS TO HARRY. CAN'T TAKE CARE OF HIMSELF. PLEASE CALL 704-343-9002. Ada touched her finger to the flier, which she saw was on poles and trees all down the block. If she had eaten her breakfast already, she most certainly would have tossed it back up.

Ada was dripping wet by the time she got back inside her living room. She closed and locked the front door and leaned her weight against it, her forehead leaving a slick mark on the wood. "Cam," she said aloud, "oh, Cam honey, I've done something wicked."

It wasn't like Cam answered her, or that Ada expected her to. But sometimes the quiet in the house felt like a pillow coming down over her face, and she needed to talk to someone.

Ada couldn't think of touching her cereal, so she covered it and put it aside. As she was struggling with the sheet of Saran Wrap, she noticed through the back window that the door to her daddy's chicken coop was wide open again. He'd kept laying hens when Ada and her brothers were young, until a hawk attack decimated the flock. "I should turn it into a craft coop," Cam used to say. In their retirement, they both liked to tinker with artsy projects— Cam had taken up woodworking, and Ada tried pottery. But Cam never got around to the restoration, and after she passed, Ada let the coop stand in the yard, sagging, along with the empty tool shed.

These days, the orange tabby that slinked freely through the neighborhood had a habit of swatting the coop door open. She'd watched the cat do it, like something out of *America's Funniest Home Videos*. She sometimes found him inside, purring and cleaning himself, like he owned the place. He had no collar that she could see, so Ada wasn't sure who he belonged to, but he was well fed and purred when she was near him.

"Matt could put a lock on that coop for you," Junie offered, "or better yet, tear it down, along with that old shed. You could get a nice new vinyl shed from Lowe's. They last forever." But Ada didn't need something to last forever, and she actually didn't mind the cat. She called it Auggie, although she had no idea if it was male or female. Ada kept a few cans of cat food around, just in case the cat showed up, and now she opened one and carried it out to the coop.

At the door of the shed, though, she cried out, and almost dropped the can. Harry Finn was curled up on the shed floor in the same clothes he'd been in yesterday, trying in vain to sleep off a bad case of dementia.

Ada remembered her dream, shaking him over and over asking if he was dead. Thankfully the question didn't need asking: His snoring sounded like a chainsaw or some other piece of equipment.

"Mr. Finn!" she said, nudging him with her index finger until his eyes opened. "This just isn't safe. You can't stay in my chicken coop!"

Harry sat up, wiping away the thin line of drool that had escaped his lips. "Sorry," he muttered. "The door was wide open and I couldn't find . . ." But his memory failed him again.

"Come on," she said, tugging at his arm to urge him up. "Your folks are looking for you."

Harry drew his arm back, flinching at the word *folks*. He seemed to be rooted, and she couldn't drag him up onto his feet.

"What if I don't want to go back?" he said, clear as a school bell. "Could you . . . If I gave you some money, would you help me get a bus ticket to Pittsburgh?"

"Is someone mistreating you?"

"No, no, *no!*" he said, frowning. "I just . . . I don't know what I'm supposed to be *doing*. I want to go *home!*"

She heard similar complaints every time she went to the senior center—the pining for homes that had been sold years before, the confusion over what to do with the remainder of lives that had gone on a bit too long. "This is the worst cruise I've ever been on," one woman had said to Ada last Christmas, as they watched a marathon showing of *It's a Wonderful Life* while sipping cranberry juice cocktail and snacking on sugar cookies.

In a way, the end of life *was* a terrible cruise. Days that had once been full of students and learning, of quiet suppers with Cam and weekend parties with friends, were now just extended naps with meals in between. Twig had passed suddenly the year before, probably a heart attack. Shirley Ann had moved to Atlanta to be with family, and even Ada's brother Foster had retired to Florida. At least Ada had her home and she knew where it was—that was a comfort. Lord willing, someday she'd die there, in her bed, Cam coming to her in a dazzling white light to lead the way.

"I understand, Mr. Finn," she said to Harry, holding out her hand to him. "I surely do. I wish I could help you. But right now, all I can do is reunite you with your daughter. She is sick with worry, just sick. Nobody deserves that, now do they?"

Inside, he slurped down the bowl of Cheerios with banana that she hadn't been able to eat, while Ada dialed the number on the flier. "My name is Ada Shook," she said to the agitated voice that answered the phone. "I live on Card Street in North . . . in NoDa. Mr. Harry Finn is in my kitchen right now eating some cereal. He's fine, looks like."

§ § §

Mimi Finn was probably in her late forties or early fifties, with freshly trimmed salt and pepper hair and crisp, preppy-style clothes like Cam used to wear—pressed khakis and a yellow polo shirt. She had inherited her father's sapphire eyes. Ada found herself trying to stand taller and straighter, and patting her hair into place like a young woman, like she was someone Mimi Finn would actually notice. "Vanity, thy name is Ada," Cam used to tease when she was too long in front of the mirror.

Mimi grabbed her father and hugged him to her like he was a life vest. "I will never let you out of my sight again! Oh my God, Dad, I was absolutely terrified!" When she released him, he ran a hand through his hair in what seemed like a nervous habit. "I don't know how to begin to thank you, Mrs. Shook."

"Miss Shook," she corrected. "Or just Ada."

Before she even realized she was hatching an idea, Ada added, "I was thinking, if you'd consider letting him out of your sight, maybe he could accompany me to the senior center. They show movies most afternoons on a nice big television, but I don't fancy going alone. It's free, and it's a way to pass the time. You like movies, Mr. Finn?"

"Some, I guess," he said.

149

"He doesn't know his way around here. He's only been with us a few months. And he doesn't have a driver's license anymore."

"I still drive everywhere," Ada said. "How 'bout I see what's showing tomorrow?"

Harry smiled, like she'd just handed him his bus ticket. But by tomorrow he probably wouldn't remember the invitation—he might not even recall her face or name when she came to fetch him. She wasn't sure it really mattered very much.

When father and daughter left, Ada heard her stomach grumbling, and she made herself a fried egg and a slice of toast. As she was mopping up the last smear of yolk, a blur of orange caught her eye through the kitchen screen door. The tabby was back and had settled on a sunny patch of grass, where he was cleaning his paws one by one with luxurious slowness.

Ada stared at him through the screen door, until he became aware of her, too, and stopped his business in mid-lick. Then she retrieved the can of food she'd opened for him earlier, and emptied it into a bowl. The hinges moaned when she threw the door open. "Here, Auggie," she beckoned. "There's a good boy."

Her Story

2015

In her eighty-first year, Ada preferred not to encounter anything out of the ordinary on a daily basis. Every Wednesday and Friday afternoon at 1:30 p.m., she drove her Buick the five blocks to Mimi Finn's house, pulled up behind the metallic blue Subaru in the driveway, and tapped her horn three times in a crisp staccato.

On the final honk, Mimi opened the door to the house and Harry was always standing in the frame, dressed just as he was when Ada first spotted him in front of her bungalow, looking like he had mislaid something. His standard uniform included a Steelers T-shirt (he surely had a bureau full of them), cuffed trousers, white sneakers, and when it was really hot, as it was most summer days in Charlotte, a baseball cap with a big *P* emblazoned on it. It was comforting that Harry looked pretty much the same every time Ada saw him.

"You two fasten your seat belts," Mimi instructed, fussing like a mother on her child's first day of school. Ada and Harry nodded, although they never clicked their belts into place for the ten-minute drive to the senior center. "They wrinkle you to high heaven," Ada said to Harry. Besides, she'd had only one serious car accident in fifty-some years of driving, if you didn't count close scrapes and fender-benders, and it was so long ago the exact circumstances had clouded over. Ada did remember that it involved a red pickup and that the collision was soon after Cam passed, when vehicles just seemed to come at her out of nowhere. She and the truck driver escaped without a scratch, although shards of glass fell out of the pockets of her pedal pushers that night, and her Buick was in the repair shop for two weeks.

Harry wasn't much in the way of company, but he was familiar to her now, like the theme song of a TV show she found herself humming later in the day. She could say just about anything to him and trust he wouldn't repeat it, because he was unlikely to recollect what she said from one hour to the next.

As the weeks went on and their trips to the center became second nature to them both, Harry stopped looking at her funny every time she pulled up to fetch him. Sometimes on their drive, he even initiated a conversation, mostly about the weather or the movies they saw. "That was some crazy movie," was a common observation of his, especially about the newer comedies starring actors neither of them had heard of. Ada's personal favorites were the classic romances and musicals, but the senior center had an eclectic collection, based on whatever DVDs folks had donated.

"What didn't you like about it?" she asked, although she knew it was a hard question for Harry, whose dementia was slipping from mild to moderate, according to Mimi. Generally, the question just sat there between them like an extra passenger, and Ada filled in the silence with her own ruminations. "I didn't think they needed all the cussing," Ada might say to Harry. Other movies had endings that were "a little too depressing for my taste."

Then one Friday, when she deposited Harry back home after a viewing of *The Sting* ("You know, you look a little like Paul Newman around the eyes," she told him) Mimi asked her in for supper, or "dinner," as she called it, and Ada's routine cracked open.

"I've been meaning to ask you for quite a while, but we're always so busy. I'm just so grateful to you, Miss Shook. You saved my father from who knows what fate." Mimi shuddered. "I don't even like to think about what could have happened to him, wandering the neighborhood, not knowing where he lives. And now, well, you're saving *me*—getting him out of the house twice a week so I can finish my work!" Mimi was a reporter for a local magazine, but she worked from home a lot, and her schedule seemed to have quite a bit of room in it.

Ada cast her eyes to her navy blue Keds. She wouldn't know what to say to a reporter and her partner, who was a university dean of something or other. Twenty or even fifteen years ago she would have found conversation easier—Cam would have been there with her comfortable manner that made strangers describe her as easy-going. Cam would never turn down an invitation, but Ada's inclination was to do just that, to retreat to her recliner as she did every night of the week. But then she pictured the frozen turkey dinner waiting for her at home. The prospect of something home-cooked made her mouth water, and she found herself accepting in spite of her misgivings.

She had to go home first, she explained, to feed her cat. It was true that the tabby expected his meals at a set time, but her real intention was to gussy herself up a little, change out of the simple blue gingham whose pockets she had reinforced at the corners. She couldn't even remember the last time she'd been invited out.

At home, she put on a favorite dress, a simple cream piqué with a twisting vine of strawberries printed at the hemline, which Cam had picked out at Belk's years back. Ada only wore it a few Sundays a year, so it was still in good shape if out of style, longer and fuller than dresses were now. She dabbed a touch of pink on her lips, and took a brush through her hair fifty times, the way she did when she was young. Her chestnut locks had once been a crown of glory, but after her hair went white, she had it cut into a manageable chin-length bob. "Nothing's worse than an old woman still trying to look young," she told the hairdresser.

Cam hadn't approved of the cut. "Can't run my hands through it now," she had said, though at the time they hadn't made proper love in years.

Ada reappeared at Mimi's at the appointed time, not a minute too early or late, and rang the old-fashioned doorbell, the kind that twisted like a crank and that Ada hadn't seen since she was a girl.

"Welcome, Miss Shook!" A sturdy woman with a halo of

blonde hair opened the door, a blast of cool air escaping onto the porch. She was wearing short shorts that emphasized her chunky legs, and a T-shirt with a map of North Carolina made out of rainbow stripes. Her handshake was as firm as a man's. "I'm Lisbeth Sorenson, Mimi's wife." Her casual use of the word *wife* set butterflies to flight in Ada's stomach. She knew women could marry each other now, but she hadn't met anyone who'd actually done so.

"Please just call me Ada," she said. "Miss Shook was the librarian at Central Junior High about a million years ago."

That brought a beam of pleasure to Lisbeth's face, which went much deeper than her lips. She was older than she looked, from the elaborate web of lines at the corners of her eyes and mouth.

Harry was watching TV at a high decibel in the living room: "I'll take World History for 400, Alex." *Jeopardy!* had been Cam's favorite show, and Ada had been unable to watch it since she passed. Alex Trebek had aged a lot in the years that had gone by, but she saw he was still a handsome man.

"Harry, Miss Shook . . . Ada is here," Lisbeth said, and Harry looked up, confused at seeing his companion in a different place and a different context.

"Is it time for a movie?"

"She's joining us for dinner, Harry. Ada, let me set your purse over here and we'll go out to the deck. It's nice and shady, and I have some *vinho verde* on ice." Ada had no idea what that was, but she hoped it was fruity so she could actually bear to drink it. She said she'd like to keep her pocketbook with her. It would give her something to hold onto, she thought.

Mimi was in the kitchen, checking the oven. A whiff of an unfamiliar dish met Ada's nostrils, and she hoped it wasn't something exotic that she'd have to push around her plate and pretend to eat. But Harry didn't seem like a man of unusual tastes, and they were feeding him, too, so Ada took heart. "I hope you like fish," Mimi said, and Ada replied she did. Which was mostly true, although she probably hadn't eaten real fish, something other than fish sticks, since she and Cam had last been to Folly

Beach. With any luck, it would be a fish she recognized and that didn't still have its head on.

Despite the heat of the day, their back yard was a cool oasis, overflowing with more colors than Ada had ever seen outside of a nursery. Differently shaped flowerbeds ringed a swimming pool with a cool turquoise floor, and a pool house was a miniature version of the main building. "Oh!" Ada exclaimed. "What a delightful yard!"

"I love to fuss with it," Lisbeth said, pouring something fizzy into a wine glass and dropping two fresh raspberries into it. "If Mimi were in charge, the yard would be a jungle."

"My . . . Cam was the same way," Ada said, taking the drink. "She always said her thumbs were black, not green." The bubbles in the drink were subtle and not as tickly as champagne. "I have a couple of small flowerbeds. It's harder on my back than it used to be to keep them up, but that's how I stay fit." Her free hand went automatically to her belly. Most of the ladies at the senior center had paunches like old men, but Ada prided herself on her trim physique.

"Were you together a long time? You and your partner?"

Partner was a more familiar word to Ada than *wife*, but she had never used either in talking about Cam. In their rather small gay circle, she said *lover*. In mixed company, it was always just *friend*. Cam had passed before couples started getting married in Massachusetts, but she lived long enough to be excited by the prospect.

"I wish I could hold on just a little longer, darlin'," she had said, close to the end. "I'd make an honest woman of you."

Cam's face came into clear view as Ada answered Lisbeth's question, but she didn't need a prompt to call it up. It shadowed her night and day. "Forty-five years. Her name was Camellia Mae Lively, but everyone just called her Cam."

"What a great Southern name!" Mimi commented as she passed by, carrying plates to the redwood table. "Was she from here, too?"

"No, Davidson," Ada said. Images from that traumatic Christmas visit to Davidson surfaced—Ada's one and only time in the Lively house—and she pushed them quickly aside.

"I would love to see pictures of the two of you," Mimi continued. "I bet you have some good ones."

"I could run home and get my album."

"Oh, no need to trouble yourself. Let's save that for next time." The phrase *next time* sent chills up both of Ada's arms. She very much wanted there to be a next time, and a time after that, a new pattern of having "dinner" in this cool, elegant yard. Just sitting on their deck, admiring the garden with a glass of something fizzy in her hand, made her feel like an adult again, someone who socialized with educated people. Too many other folks these days raised their voices and enunciated more clearly when she was around, even though her hearing was fine, her mind as sharp as a fish hook. "I'm old, not deaf," she'd snapped at the pharmacist just last week.

Mimi served the flakiest white fish she'd ever tasted— sheepshead, she called it, from the coast. Harry's version was plain with a side of buttered broccoli and a baked potato, but Ada's helping came on a bed of something smooth and creamy, almost like puréed grits, with a mound of tangy greens on the side. Lisbeth poured more wine with the meal. Ada didn't drink it, but she scooped out the raspberries with her spoon and let them melt on her tongue.

She never drank, and her head soon felt like fluffy cotton. In between bites she talked, more than she remembered doing in years. These new friends actually asked her questions about herself, especially Mimi; must be the reporter in her. If Ada hadn't had a bubbly drink, she might have thought the questions nosy, or rude, even; but in her slightly giddy state, she took them as welcome interest.

Tea and a custardy dessert followed dinner, but Harry turned up his nose and went back inside. "I'll get you some ice cream, Harry," Lisbeth offered, following him in, and Mimi and Ada found themselves alone on the deck.

"You know, Ada, I had an ulterior motive in asking you here,"

Mimi said with a grin. "I mentioned to you that I'm a feature writer for *Charlotte Magazine.*"

"I've seen it at the library," Ada said, although she had only recently shown interest in the slick magazine, especially the byline "M.M. Finn."

"So here's the thing. I pitched a story to my editor about you."

Ada stopped in mid-sip so she wouldn't spit tea on her dress. Magazine stories were about famous people and criminals. She had done nothing to make herself famous, and she knew for a fact that sodomy was no longer a crime in North Carolina. Cam had lived to see the Supreme Court ruling and had read the story aloud to Ada. "Darlin'," she said with a catch in her voice, "looks like we're no longer outlaws." They exchanged a quick kiss and as they pulled apart, shared a look that said they were both thinking about Auggie, even though neither of them mentioned his name.

"Why ever would you want to write about me?" Ada asked Mimi as she regained her composure. It sounded too clipped, especially after she'd just been a guest at Mimi's table, so she added, "I mean, I'm nobody."

"Don't say that! I know I'm a bit biased, but you are a genuine hero. You found my father after he was missing for almost a full day!"

"Oh," Ada said, "there's no story there."

"Well, the story wouldn't be *that*, of course. You're a hero in so many other ways! It would be about your life growing up right here in an old Charlotte mill community. You could tell some of the stories you told us tonight, like when NoDa was North Charlotte, or about working at a local school during integration and busing, being gay before Stonewall, your friend Auggie's ordeal, caring for your father and then your partner . . . I can't believe how much you've experienced. You're like a time capsule of the twentieth century!" Mimi's hands waved wildly as she became more and more animated. "We could run it next August, to coincide with the Pride Festival. I know folks involved with that—maybe you could be honored somehow, or maybe Lisbeth could get you an appearance at the university. What do you think?"

Had she really told Mimi all those personal details? She guessed she had been a bit too chatty as she tried to keep up her end of the conversation.

"I think . . . I'd . . . rather not," Ada said, dragging out the words so she wouldn't tread on Mimi's pride.

Mimi's eyes registered surprise. Ada wondered if she'd be embarrassed, or worse, by having to tell her editor the story wasn't a done deal.

"I live alone," Ada added. "I don't want to advertise."

Lisbeth walked back onto the deck with a pitcher of ice water and refilled everyone's glasses.

"You know, I could be discreet about you and Miss Lively . . . if you want," Mimi continued, like she was handing back a fifty-dollar bill she had found on the sidewalk. "Or better yet, I could obscure the neighborhood you're in."

"I don't want to be any bother."

Mimi took a deep breath, still not giving up. "It wouldn't take too much of your time, if that's what concerns you. A few hours for the interview, tops, including the photo shoot. We could do the whole thing right here in the garden. Maybe you would do me the honor of letting me buy you a new dress for the occasion."

Ada fidgeted in her chair, her best dress suddenly feeling like a hand-me-down.

"Honey, it doesn't sound like Ada wants to," Lisbeth said. A look passed between the two women that Ada recognized. She'd given Cam many looks just like that in their decades together, taken the same firm tone even while softening the rebuke with "honey."

"Well, I don't see why not," Mimi said, sounding bossy and annoyed for the first time since Ada had met her. It was a peek into her personality that Ada hadn't counted on. She thought again of Cam, how she could rile Ada up quicker than anybody. "Please, at least say you'll consider it. Sleep on it. Maybe give me your final answer next time you pick up Dad."

Final answer echoed in her mind, like she was a contestant on *Who Wants to Be a Millionaire?* But there was no prize that Ada could see for anyone but Mimi herself. The taste of fish rose in her throat.

"I need to use the ladies'," she said.

"Oh, Ada, you look terrible! Let me help you," Lisbeth offered.

Lisbeth's hand supported her arm as they made their way down a long corridor, much too long to belong to one of the old mill houses. It was like they'd added another full house onto the original. Ada wondered if she would make it to the bathroom in time.

"I'll be fine," she insisted, closing the door on Lisbeth's panic. Ada lifted the toilet lid, bent over the cool porcelain, and heaved, but nothing came out.

"Ada? Do you need help?"

"I do not! Just leave me . . . please." Ada closed the lid and sat down heavily, hot tears rolling down her cheeks. She wasn't sure what made her sadder, the idea that Mimi was just trying to use her, or the fact that the flicker of hope she'd felt all evening had been so rudely extinguished.

When she opened the door finally, Lisbeth was gone and Mimi was standing in her place. Her face looked like someone had opened a tap and drained the color out of it. "Ada," she said in a small, cracked voice, "I am so, so sorry. I didn't realize how . . ."

"I'm not fragile, if that's what you think," Ada interrupted. "I'm not a scared old lady. I've been through more than you can imagine and lived to tell the tale. I just . . . we were friends, I thought. I was wrong. I feel a bit foolish."

"No, no, you weren't wrong! Lisbeth and I are very fond of you."

"How could you be? You don't know me."

"I would like to know you better."

"Why, so you can write about me?" Ada snapped. "Show me off to your editor, or at Lisbeth's school, like some prize pig?"

"I wasn't thinking . . ."

"I know you weren't. All that crazy talk about me being a hero!

159

It's not heroic just to *live!*" Some spittle escaped her lips. *Do you have to be so goddamn dramatic, Ada Jane? The woman's trying to pay you a compliment,* Cam's voice said in her head. Ada rummaged in her bag for a tissue to blot her mouth.

Mimi's eyes looked even bluer than before and watery, like her own tears were fixing to spill out. "No disrespect, Ada, but I have to contradict you. It *is* heroic to live as yourself when it's 1960 and the whole culture is saying you shouldn't be who you are. You're right—I can't imagine all you've endured that I never had to. In my mind, a woman like you ought to be celebrated and held up as a beacon. I apologize for being so pushy about the article, but I don't regret asking."

Something shifted inside her just then, and Ada held Mimi's gaze. She had never thought about her life, or Cam's, in that way, that what they had been through might be of value to another generation. They had just gotten by as best they could and been thankful for the years they had together.

She reached out and took Mimi's arm, and they walked back to the garden together in silence. Lisbeth had turned on strings of white lights whose reflection danced in the pool like stars. Over a second cup of tea, Ada allowed herself to wonder how it would be to have her picture in a magazine, or to talk to students again—this time not as a spinster librarian, but as someone with a real story to tell.

She reckoned she could find a new dress on sale at Belk's.

About the Author

Paula Martinac is the author of three other published novels—the Lambda Literary Award-winning *Out of Time* (1990; 2012 e-book); the Lammy-nominated *Home Movies* (1993); and *Chicken* (1997; 2001 reprint). She also co-authored a short story collection, *Voyages Out* (1989), with Carla Tomaso.

Paula's other publications include three nonfiction books—notably, *The Queerest Places: A National Guide to Gay and Lesbian Historic Sites* (1997)—and numerous articles, essays and short stories on LGBT themes. She wrote the biweekly column "Lesbian Notions" on LGBT politics and culture from 1997 to 2005, which was syndicated in the LBGT press.

Also a playwright, Paula's plays have had productions with Pittsburgh Playwrights Theater Company, Manhattan Theatre Source, the Pittsburgh New Works Festival, the Ganymede Festival, No Name Players, and others. Her full-length screenplay, *Foreign Affairs*, about the love affair between journalist Dorothy Thompson and novelist Christa Winsloe, finished second place in the 2003 POWER UP screenwriting contest.

Originally from Pittsburgh, Paula spent most of her adult life in New York City before boomeranging back to Pittsburgh for eleven years. In 2014, she and her wife, writer and professor Katie Hogan, moved to Charlotte, N.C., where Paula teaches creative writing to undergraduates at the University of North Carolina at Charlotte.

For more, please visit www.paulamartinac.com

Acknowledgments

My neighborhood started as a cotton mill community in Charlotte, N.C. in the early 1900s. Transplants like me abound, but there are also native Charlotteans who have been here for decades, holding on to their tiny mill houses and plots of land. One day after I'd taken a walk and spotted an older woman tending her azaleas, a funny thing happened: A character named Ada Jane Shook, whom I imagined growing up a mill worker's daughter, appeared in a story I was writing about an old man from Pittsburgh. I pictured her living in the house she'd grown up in, just a few streets over from mine. At first I mistook her for a heterosexual widow, but she quickly set me *straight.* I am grateful for the opportunity to tell her story.

Two different writing groups read these stories over the course of many months. I've been with East End Writers since 2003, although it's now a Skype group because of geographic distance. Thank you, Selene dePackh, Kristie Linden, and Lucy Turner for your friendship and your spot-on recommendations that have made this a stronger book . . . and for always saying, "Yay, another Ada story!"

To be told "You'd never know you were from the North" is the highest praise I could have gotten for this particular book. Thank you to my Charlotte-based writers' group—Ana Couch, Debra Efird, Wendy Oglesby, and Shari Tate—for your astute comments. Not to mention all the perks that come with a face-to-face group, like the most delicious king cake I've ever tasted.

For help with earlier versions of two of these chapters, thanks to the editors at *Raleigh Review* and *Minerva Rising,* for their insightful edits for "Comfort Zone" and "Raised That Way," respectively.

My own work has benefited enormously from teaching creative writing to undergraduates at the University of North Carolina at Charlotte. Many thanks to the English Department for making me feel at home.

For help at different stages in my research, I'd like to acknowledge Reed Williams, who offered insight into a typical workday for a school librarian. Larry Nix of LibraryHistoryBuff.org pointed me toward information about educational requirements and certification for school librarians in the 1950s.

My experience working with Bywater Books on the e-book reprint of my first novel, *Out of Time,* was so positive that I knew Ada and Cam would feel right at home there. Warmest thanks to Marianne K. Martin, Kelly Smith, and Salem West for taking on this book; Ann McMan for the best cover ever; Rachel Spangler for her social media insights; and Caroline Curtis and Nancy Squires for careful copy editing and proofreading. And thank you, Michele Karlsberg, for inviting me to Bywater in 2012.

Finally, this book is for Katie Hogan, my partner in crime since 1992 and lawfully wedded wife since 2014, who gave me the incredible gift of a sabbatical from working multiple jobs so that I could write fiction again. But she did even more than that: If I so much as hinted I was having trouble with an Ada story, she took time out of her own demanding work and academic writing schedule to help me sort it out. I love you, and I love what we've built together.

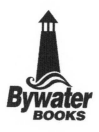

Bywater
BOOKS

At Bywater Books we love good books about lesbians just like you do, and we're committed to bringing the best of contemporary lesbian writing to our avid readers. Our editorial team is dedicated to finding and developing outstanding writers who create books you won't want to put down.

We sponsor the Bywater Prize for Fiction to help with this quest. Each prizewinner receives $1,000 and publication of their novel. We have already discovered amazing writers like Jill Malone, Sally Bellerose, and Hilary Sloin through the Bywater Prize. Which exciting new writer will we find next?

For more information about Bywater Books and the annual Bywater Prize for Fiction, please visit our website.

www.bywaterbooks.com